OUR SHADOWS' VOICE

Douglas W. Milliken

Fomite
Burlington, VT

An early version of "Cast in Water, 1982" appeared as part of the interactive online media piece "Ben Nigra, 1982," co-produced by Andrew Lyman and released by Nada Publishing.

ISBN- 978-1-944388-83-6
Library of Congress Number- 2018967928

Fomite
58 Peru Street
Burlington, VT 05439
www.fomitepress.com

stranger: the extraction of an inner warmth we always hoped was there.

—Meghan Lamb, author of *All Your Most Private Places* and S*ilk Flowers*

Milliken's immersive fiction always takes us to places we may be afraid to look. *Blue of the World* continues that trend. Beneath the lucid, serene surface of the prose lies disturbing realities. Instead of pretending to hold the answers to life's complexity, Milliken invites us to celebrate the beauty of unsettling mystery. The characters throughout the collection strike a unique balance between loneliness and hope. I emerged from the last page ultimately feeling less alone, more hopeful, and profoundly grateful to live in a world where these stories exist.

—Nat Baldwin, author of *The Red Barn*

Douglas W. Milliken's characters navigate the vast and the intimate, in love, panic, and despair, and even in the most ordinary moments. Milliken is a master of leveling that field of experience and revealing the things we all carry with us—awe, insecurity, nostalgia—whether we're looking up at the stars or about to be swept out to sea

—Celia Johnson, Creative Director, SLICE Literary

Praise for *One Thousand Owls Behind Your Chest*

One of Portland's most prolific and original fiction writers.
—*The Portland Dispatch*

In Milliken's stories, you get characters who seem like regular-ass people until their motivations […] collide them.
—*The Portland Phoenix*

Praise for *To Sleep as Animals*

A disturbance of a very specific flavor […] Milliken's writing is urgent yet finely considered—a literate pleasure.
—Carl Skoggard, translator of *Walter Benjamin's Berlin Childhood circa 1900*

A distinctive and often vertiginously frightening psychological landscape […] bracingly disturbing.
—Megan Grumbling, author of *Persephone in the Late Anthropocene*

Also by Douglas W. Milliken

White Horses
To Sleep as Animals
Brand New Moon
Cream River
One Thousand Owls Behind Your Chest
Monolith (with Cat Bates)
The Opposite of Prayer
In the Mines (with Scott Sell)
Blue of the World

In memory of J.S., D.M., & G.B.

In theory these mementos serve to bring back the moment.
In fact they serve only to make clear how inadequately I
appreciated the moment when it was here.
How inadequately I appreciated the moment when it was
here is something else I could never afford to see.

—Joan Didion, Blue Nights

CONTENTS

Cast in Water
1982

A BOOTPRINT SUNK IN CREEKBED MUCK. THE WHISPERING SHUSH of dead leaves. A slice of afternoon sunlight pouring through parted curtains to illuminate wandering airborne dust. The call-and-response of laughter in the woods, in a field, in class. A board game unfolded on a glossy hardwood floor. Pieces scattered like ash. Ben Nigra's memory is a spray of broken glass, candy-apple red and green, soldered together by association—by however the fragments can possibly fit—into a stained-glass image of a little boy playing among dead leaves under a severe autumn sky. Sun burning white the sheet-iron clouds. Ben's memory is a mosaic of Joshua Sams.

JOSHUA SAMS. OF THE SUMMER–SUN BLEACHED RINGLETS AND sun-pink knuckle of nose. Of the perpetual laughter-in-waiting. Of the excellence in mathematics. Of Ms. Fiori's constant chagrin. Of the ivy-and-brick townhouse near the public library, the third-floor apartment, the tall narrow windows and polished sock-slippery floors. Of the dark-haired, dark-eyed mother with whom a furtive smile was a gift and trait in common. Of the father like a blonde ox in seersucker and smeared glasses. Of the older sister like a distant promise. Joshua Sams, who Ben did not know and then suddenly did know—in the first few weeks of the third grade—then just as suddenly did not know and could never know again.

Joshua Sams. There and gone like lightning in the night, imprinting its ghost against memory and eye. A convincing mirage in the fall of 1982.

AND THOUGH OF COURSE THEY HAD TO HAVE MET FIRST— nothing can begin until they have met—everything begins for Ben in Joshua Sams' apartment, outside Joshua's bedroom, both boys kneeling on the hallway floor while somewhere in the kitchen, Joshua's mother quietly sang some strange and elusive melody. While the father read a paper in his recliner in the den. While the sister engaged in something unknown behind her closed bedroom door. They were playing with Joshua's new action figures, whose joints articulated and whose molded hands held weapons of amazing firepower. And the light through the windows was sleepy and afternoon bright, igniting the stocking-slid-ing polished wood floors, illuminating each falling mote of dust. And for one second the sun sank to its singular most crucial degree, an angle perfect and refined so that every-thing shined bright and radiant. As if their play war was enacted in a wash of pure light. As if all the world were light. The sun ignited its blinding fuse, and within it, they were lost.

Or the opposite ritual of afternoons after school, playing not at Joshua's but in the woods behind Ben's house. They would walk the extra blocks through the more sparsely-housed avenues, through a field of chest-high grass to the slowly yellowing reddening oranging woods, the eventually denuding birches and maples, to play make-believe games alongside the creek, water burbling mindlessly over stone.

Already by this time, Ben had given up on collecting toys. His parents still sometimes bought things for him that they thought he might enjoy, but it was like they were buying gifts for a boy who no longer existed. What was the point in collecting these things predestined for loss or eventual disuse? In the woods by the creek, Joshua and Ben played with sticks and rocks and the implements conjured of their own imaginations.

Friends and toys: both things destined for loss. Another unique feature of Joshua Sams. Ben associated with no other children at school.

Or sometimes they'd eschew the streets in favor of the old railroad tracks—deeply rusted red with neglect, a forgotten toy of an older generation—taking the longer route through the woods and field until the tracks crossed a dirt road that ran near Ben's house. They would take the longer path to play in the woods along the creek, and sometimes on this railway trail they would pass older kids on the tracks, mostly boys but sometimes girls and always at least one of them smoking. Sometimes the older kids would tease Ben and Joshua as they passed, their tone only semi-joking. More often, though, they were ignored. They were always allowed to pass.

BUT MAYBE IT'S NOT IMPORTANT HOW THEY MET. WITHOUT A beginning, how can there be an end? Ben's memory can be a time capsule, an object completely removed from all other facets of his life. A precursor, empty of shared context or experience. It could be a separate small eternity unto itself wherein each afternoon drifted into evening's dusk while their make-believe games by the creek inevitably concluded with one or the other announcing that, from a rapidly closing distance—through the woods, skulking in low underbrush hoards—the goblins were coming, they must run from the night because goblins were coming. They would flee the site of their darkening games, calling retreat while spurring invisible mounts to a gallop through the tall grass. Leaving the muttering creek to fend for itself.

AT JOSHUA'S HOUSE, THERE WERE NO GOBLINS. THE MOMENT of pure and enveloping afternoon light would come and go like some rapid tide and their games would continue on the hallway floor until Joshua's mother called them for supper, their game ending as the father relinquished his paper, as the sister emerged from her room. They would eat slow and companionably in the Sams' dining room, Ben seated across from the sister and too nervous to ever say much of anything, hoping his foot might accidentally touch her foot beneath the table. Ben would eat with the Sams then walk home in the increasing indigo of evening, and no goblins were ever mentioned for there were no goblins in town. In the woods or maybe hidden under tall rocks, sure—in a desert plain or under the cliffs by the ocean or by a Great Lake—but never in town. Where streetlights lit the way. Where the paved paths could never be lost.

Joshua Sams never ate dinner with Ben and his family. The invitation was always open but never accepted. Joshua never explained why.

But the details of our lives are not switches randomly flipped on or off. We don't live and behave a certain way only to suddenly change, become someone or something new. Preferring chocolate to vanilla. Coffee to tea. Something must flip the switch.

It is important how Ben met Joshua Sams.

The day opened with the same mix of excitement and nausea that must accompany all first days of school—new clothes and faces intangibly changed by summer—but the benediction of third grade came with an extra sick thrill. Ben had been working alongside the same twenty-three boys and girls since kindergarten, and though none were friends, all were familiar, safe. This year, though, he'd be in a different class with different children. He'd be in Ms. Fiori's class. They would learn fractions and decimals while their peers in other classrooms struggled with multiplication. They would be reporting on books they chose and read on their own. They would become more autonomous in their learning.

At least this is how Ben's parents had explained it. But once the bell rang and the children filtered inside from the playground, the scene seemed exactly the same as his previous years of school. The teacher speaking slowly and smiling too much. The children fidgeting and picking their noses when they thought no one could see. The faint scent of peanut butter, pencil shavings, and child sweat. The faces had changed, but nothing else.

But what change could he expect? People were machines. Their bodies grew, but their programming remained the same. This, Ben knew. This, Ben seemed to have always known.

The morning's events swam through the hours until lunch and recess and it was only after this midday break, during the first science lesson of the year, that Ben became aware of Joshua Sams. Half of the students were given small nets like those used in pet stores to scoop fish from an aquarium. The other half were given Mason jars with a constellation of holes punched through the lids. The children were all paired off and led to the big downward sloping field behind the school. Ben was paired with Joshua Sams.

The objective of the lesson, Ms. Fiori explained, was to gather up an insect in the net, then transfer it to the jar, where they then could examine the insect and take notes on its appearance and behavior before releasing it again into the wind-swishing field.

"Don't just trap up the first bug you find," she warned as the children disbursed through the grass. "Make sure it's something you *want* to study."

Sky bright and a deep clean blue, sun warm on Ben's back, he and Joshua Sams waded through the grass, barely speaking. They spotted a cricket and a fat grey spider and finally caught a preying mantis in Joshua's net. It was young, small and twiggy brown. Yet despite its size, its posture was all threat. In short hovering bursts, it tried to fly inside its glassy cell.

"Do you think it's scared of us?" Ben asked. It was the first thing he'd directly said to Joshua. It was not yet clear to him why he'd asked.

"No." Joshua's voice was almost a whisper. As if guarding against the possibility that the mantis might overhear. "I think *he* thinks we're scared of *him*."

Somewhere in the grass around them, a girl's voice rose up in a scream. Somewhere in the grass, boys' voices laughingly bit.

"That's why we captured him." Nearly touching his nose to the jar, Ben examined the narrow body, the brittle limbs, the black oil-drop eyes. Complete in its alienness. A living unknown. Hovering below the lid, the mantis stared back in a silent seethe. "Because we *are* scared."

Joshua nodded and looked at Ben, and for the first time the two boys saw one another.

"Exactly," and he grinned. "We're terrified."

BUT WHY SHOULD FEAR BE THE TIE THAT BOUND THESE TWO together? Their families were quiet if not actually happy. In school, their noteworthilessness made them essentially invisible to the roving dull-eyed bullies. Even in terms of the occasional catcalls of faggot and kike from the smoker kids on the bridge, there was nothing to fear. Only something vaguely unpleasant. Awkward but somehow necessary. Just another social interaction.

The mantis, though, was not like these things. It was everything that they were not. Its terrifying unknowability was exciting.

Once when the descending afternoon hours turned to rain, they made the wrong decision to go to Ben's house to play. Cold and blue, empty of toys and games. Their lackluster conversation drew to a inevitable still as they lay sprawled on Ben's bedroom floor. At last, they played the game in which each pretended he was dead.

When Ben's mom came in to call them to dinner, she found two dead boys on the floor.

OR ONCE WHILE WALKING ALONG THE RAIL LINE AFTER CLASS— while discussing a book wherein a rope is a bridge and a grove is an ancient kingdom—they came out of the woods into the final stretch of field before turning toward Ben's, and along the way found the smoking teens on a low rail-bridge crossing an earlier portion of the creek. From a garbage bag held among them, the teens produced empty beer bottles to hurl and smash against the rocks below. Cold October water tripping along the broken edges. Sour greens and ruminating browns. Ben and Joshua mingled in among the teens, mostly boys but for Joshua's sister, who was not throwing glass, only watching, thoughtfully smoking.

When Joshua's sister saw Ben, she put her hand on his head. Laced her fingers through his hair. Stroked the back of his head and neck to tweak his left ear gently, not unkindly, before withdrawing her hand and turning away to gaze again into the glassy belly of the creek. The sun's light melting into her near-black hair. Spider-leg lashes framing her near-black eyes. It was the closest thing to a conversation the two had ever shared.

Meanwhile, one of the teens—a tall cow-eyed blonde who couldn't help but be on the basketball team—in orgiastic glee fished from the bag an empty can of Miller Highlife and threw it over the edge, everyone growing quiet and still to watch the can break ranks and float downstream, gold and silver bobbing to illuminate to these boys something that, upon discovery, they realized they should have known all along.

YET EVEN IF THIS WERE A CAPSULE—SEPARATE FROM PAST AND future, immune to all context beyond its own—it would need limits. Boundaries to separate it from what it's not. A necessary beginning. A necessary end.

WHEN THE CAN DISAPPEARED AROUND THE BEND, THE TEENS returned to breaking glass, determined to complete what they'd set out to destroy.

IT WAS JUST AFTER MORNING ROLL CALL, THE LAST TIME BEN saw Joshua Sams. The day was a deep and biting blue, dew balancing coolly on the edges of the grass, the chain-link fence, the cold grey metal of the monkey bars and slides. Ben's class had confirmed its presence and pledged its allegiance and was in the opening throes of the daily grammar lesson when, from behind Ben and to the right, a sound halfway between a whimper and a cough achingly punctuated the morning's chalk-dust air. Like something sharp caught painfully in a throat, unable or unwilling to move up or down.

A ragged finger icily traced the knuckles of Ben's spine. He did not turn to see the source of this sound.

But then it happened again a moment later, louder and more urgent, and this time everyone heard. The lesson stopped. All eyes turned toward a common point, and Ben was helpless but to turn too, turn and see Joshua Sams hunched over his desk, skin cheese-white and eyes glossed with tears.

"Joshua?" Ms. Fiori's voice was the dry creaking of a closing door. "Is everything all right?"

Joshua tried to answer, but his voice again was that crushed suffering sound, and this time—in the tremble of his shoulders, the tight grimace of his mouth, the pinching of his eyes—it was obvious how much pain he was holding back, holding in.

A certain straightness elongated Ms. Fiori's spine. As if someone were pulling taut a string fastened to the crown of her skull. "Would someone please volunteer to escort Joshua to the nurse's office, please?"

The double-please. A silent moment passed through the still room. From an arm's length away, Ben stared at his friend. Saw Joshua's mouth quivering with his uneven breath. Saw a single tear slide down his cheek. Joshua Sams. His only friend in the world. Yet Ben could not raise his hand.

Finally, another boy—Mark Alotta, the class's self-styled teacher's pet—volunteered, and together he and Joshua slowly rose and left the room. Mark had to help Joshua rise from his seat. Mark had to hold him to help him walk and stand. Ben wished Joshua would look back at him—if only to confirm the guilt he was already feeling, guilt he would always feel—but Joshua did not look back. The classroom door clicked open and clicked shut, and Ben never saw his friend again.

THIS WAS ON A WEDNESDAY. THURSDAY MORNING, MS. FIORI said that Joshua Sams was in the hospital, but couldn't say why. She said they could spend their morning grammar lessons making cards for Joshua, wishing him a speedy recovery. Someone would deliver the cards Friday morning to Joshua's family.

Ben worked throughout the morning and when the period was over and he still wasn't done, he asked Ms. Fiori if he could finish the card at home, bring it in first thing in the morning. It didn't seem like her mouth wanted to work. It took a while for her to finally say okay.

THAT AFTERNOON, BEN DID NOT GO DOWN TO THE CREEK BEHIND his house. The few leaves left clinging to the branches were yellow or brown and limp. They did nothing to hide the hunched shadows moving between the trees.

Ben watched the woods from his bedroom window until the sun set early and it became too dark to see. Then he finished his friend's card.

JOSHUA'S SISTER DISAPPEARED FROM SCHOOL ALMOST AS SOON as Joshua did. Ben wished he could see her, could talk to her, find out how his friend was, but he knew he wouldn't know how to ask, wouldn't know what to say. He imagined that somehow the two of them being together might be some kind of comfort. He imagined that she'd place her hand in his hair again.

But of course, she wasn't around for this to happen. Ben walked to and from school, searching, alone, walked the playground alone.

BEN'S CARD WAS IN FULL COLOR, IF IN A LIMITED SPECTRUM: yellow to birches, orange and red to maples, a fat purple blade to the ashes. Mottled trunks of white and grey ending before they reached the ground. But Friday morning, he was not asked for his card. After attendance and the pledge of allegiance, Ms. Fiori stood and read a letter from Joshua's parents wherein they thanked the class for their thoughts and concerns and prayers and for the friendship the children had given their son. Wherein they expressed their sorrow, explaining how Joshua had fallen into a deep sleep Wednesday night and did not wake up, how by noon the next day his heart had stopped moving and his lungs had given up. Wherein they wished that everyone who wanted to could come to the funeral, but because of their family's and their culture's traditions, Joshua had to be buried immediately. The funeral would be taking place later this morning.

The letter closed with Joshua's parents again giving thanks, though for what, Ben didn't know. Then Ms. Fiori set down the letter and instructed everyone to put away their books, for they were now to be tested on spelling.

ONE TIME, JOSHUA BEAT BEN AT A GAME OF CHECKERS BY taking six pieces in a single turn.

One time, they jumped out of a closet to scare Ben's mom, then stood hangdog and sick-feeling when they saw they'd made her cry.

OR AFTER THE FALL'S LAST HEAVY RAIN, WHEN THE CREEK GREW fat and fast, swelling over the banks, and they took off their clothes and swam, gasping with laughter as the cold water wet them with its winter-toothed tongue, stealing their breath.

OR WHEN THEY CLIMBED A TREE AND FORGOT HOW TO CLIMB DOWN.

THE MANTIS CLAMBERED ABOUT AND AGAIN TRIED TO FLY BUT mostly stood still in an awkward pugilist's pose while Joshua and Ben took notes on its body, its structure and behavior, aware of the fear that gave birth to their curiosity and aware of conquering their fears.

THOUGH RECORDS INDICATE THAT HE SCORED AN A‑ (*cabbadge, turnup*), Ben does not remember taking his spelling test. He does not remember the lessons in reading, in grammar, in division and multiplication. He does not remember eating lunch. All Ben remembers is again and again, Joshua standing and leaving for the nurse's office, leaving while Ben silently watches him go.

Ben remembers becoming aware of himself standing in the middle of the playground during noon recess. Hands hidden in the pockets of his puffy blue jacket. Children whizzing and screaming by. He remembers feeling not so much like the still immobile center of the universe around which everything spins but like the furthest, most remote of edges. Far away from the binding center of anything. Paralyzed by his distance from the world.

With the unrushed pace of the sleeping or lost, Ben fled the playground. Down the grassy slope behind the school. Through the woods to the abandoned tracks, cold and rusted red.

O R THE TIME THEY FOUND THE ABANDONED WELL FAR OUT IN
the wild belly of the woods. Blowdowns leaning drunk-
enly against other trees or collapsed fully among the
fallen leaves and underbrush. Clawing thorns and scraggly
limbs. They were racing through the maze of understory
thicket and all at once, there it was. A black open maw of
stone and timbers dropping straight down into the earth.
The faint mineral smell of water. A cold slow breath. They
stared deep into the well for a long time. Then Joshua
found a stone, threw it down and in, found others and
threw those in and Ben found and threw stones, too.
They would throw a stone, and lean low, and listen. Heads
tipped into the well. Breath caught fast in their throats.
But no matter how many times they tried, they never once
heard a stone touch bottom.

L ATER THAT NIGHT WHEN B EN FINALLY CAME HOME, HIS MOM
put on a record from her collection—something by Bob
Dylan about a man who was born in the desert and lived in
the desert and was finally gunned down in the black desert
night—and sat on the couch with him in their dark living
room. His head in her lap and her hand in his hair. His
mom didn't say anything about his dirty boots on the couch.

When the first side of the record ended, Ben's dad
wordlessly came in and turned the disc over, reset the
needle, then joined them on the couch by Ben's feet.
Unlaced and shucked off Ben's boots. Squeezed his cold
wet feet until they were pink and warm again.

Later, his mom poured him a warm bath. Later still,

his dad read to him as Ben lay in bed, silent and sleepless and still.

The book was about a boy who lived behind a gas station with his father, who hunted pheasants with poisoned fruit. Ben's dad lay beside him and read until drifting off in midsentence. Ben waited, then turned out the light, watched the darkness expanding against the ceiling while beside him, his dad breathed the long deep breaths of sleep.

BEN WALKED THE TRACKS FOR HOURS, LOSING TRACK OF TIME and himself among the denuded trees, the creosote-stinking railway ties.

At the crossing above the creek, he stopped and stared into the water.

Flat river stones. The jagged teeth of broken glass.

Ben descended the rocky bank to wade into the cold October rush.

Bent and gathered the glass from the bottom.

Once or twice cut his hands on the glass.

Didn't notice.

Pink ribbons flashing to disappear into the current.

Ben climbed again up the bank, hands and pockets full.

To again stand at the tracks' edge above the creek.

To throw the broken glass back in.

AND THOUGH HE DOES NOT REMEMBER HOW, BEN FINALLY by mid-afternoon found himself on the high hill on the opposite side of town, far from the tracks and river and school, from everything his life so far had contained. He walked the hill with his fingertips trailing along the rock retaining wall whose capstone ran high above his head and slowly decreased along the ascent until it stood as nothing beside his walking feet, a decreasing rock wall topped with a fence of angular wrought iron—blocky bars and arrowhead-tipped—beyond which ranged the long cold acres of the town's only cemetery.

His aim was to pass through the gate before dark. Find Joshua's grave. Leave his card atop the freshly turned soil, pinned against the wind by a small river stone in his pocket. This was his plan. This is what he planned to do. To accompany his friend this far in return for not having accompanied him far enough before. But before he reached the gate, through the wrought-iron bars of the fence, he saw—several tiers away but still near enough to decipher—a pile of darkly turned earth beside a square hole cutting like an open doorway in the ground, the whole scene overlooked by a polished new stone, gleaming and well-water black.

In years to come, Ben would learn that this could not possibly be Joshua's grave. That the dead are buried immediately. That their final beds are made in advance. But seeing this scene—the open hole, the waiting soil—Ben could not proceed into the cemetery. He held onto the bars of the fence and willed himself onward but did not go onward and hated himself for his failure. In terms clearer and more well-defined than anything he had previously understood or would ever understand again.

Head hanging like a broken branch caught in the boughs of its tree, he descended the hill, away from his friend and back into town.

Along his walk in the fading cloud-light of afternoon he saw skeletons and ghosts, vampires and the Incredible Hulk. It took a while for him to remember that this weekend was Halloween.

On his way home, Ben stopped at the brick townhouse of the remaining Sams. He did not ring the bell. Simply opened the mailbox and deposited the card he had made. Colored leaves and stippled-white trunks. For a moment he stood, staring into the open mailbox with his hand in his pocket and the river stone in his hand. Then he left that, too, resting over the one word he'd written on the card, and left.

They had designed and assembled their costumes together. Ben was to be a sort of butcher-zombie, grease-smeared and paunchy with a pillow stuffed under his apron, a cardboard meat cleaver clutched in his decaying hand. He called this character "Dayud." It was something he'd seen once in a dream.

Joshua was to be a mantis.

PAST HIS HOUSE. THROUGH THE TALL GRASS. TO THE WATER running among bare trees. He sat atop a boulder overlooking the creek. Always moving, always changing. Always the same exact creek. In the muck along the shore: a single oblong hole from where Joshua had stepped and sank and sprang back, losing his boot in the wet sucking grasp. Filling from the bottom up, the hole nearly brimmed now with water. Cold and black.

Ben sat still and watched the creek. Felt a tight numbness spread from his chest into his throat. Felt it overcome his body. Inch by inch. He felt it become his body. The low sun crept among the dull curtains of clouds, darkening the afternoon's already-long shadows. The trees became black slashes against the light.

From his perch, Ben felt himself become so much less than what he'd previously been—much less than he could ever be again—and as the day became that evening's dusk, he watched them emerge as shadows from the trees, eyes gleaming wetly from among the black wood, hunched imprints negating the failing light, withered and haggard and crippled with disease: Ben watched the goblins emerge.

Fed By Ravens
1991

THE SUN WAKES SOFTLY AS A SPOT OF HAZE BURNISHING THE iron horizon. Becomes a sterling furnace above. Loses itself ultimately in deepening valley clouds as old snow hisses and slithers across the highways stretching from Western Massachusetts across the Hudson, into the glacial ruts and scars of Central New York State. Foothills and gorges. Towns with impossible names. Naomi watches the landscape emerge and dissolve through the Greyhound's blurry window glass—breath-fogged and greasy with a history of greasy hands and leaning, tired heads—insulated from the world by her parka and her headphones, by the woolen caul of her giddy sleepless vacancy. A filmstrip projection outside her window. A murmuring drone of soundtrack, voices and engine. It doesn't feel like she's going anywhere at all.

Not long after noon, the bus pulls into a fast-food chain's parking lot in the strip-mall anonymity at the edge of town, and as Naomi descends the steps into the crisp

November air, she's greeted by the scents of meat grease and diesel, by the plaintive wail of scavenging seagulls, by the warm invitation of her father's waiting arms. Thick and grinning like a friendly ox. His embrace swallows her into his mohair coat. Just long enough for her to become comfortable again in his arms. One half her creator and one half her self. Coffee and aftershave. The sharp stubble of his cheek. The softest kiss in her hair.

Eyes lost behind the clouds reflecting in his spotted glasses, he loads her bag into the trunk of his Oldsmobile.

"You've gotten taller."

"Not even a little bit."

"I know," and for a moment, her father seems legitimately disappointed. "Me neither."

Sitting sideways in the passenger seat as they drive through town, watching her father's impassive profile—ruddy and blunt-nosed and silvering at the temples—Naomi's head feels cast through with thin clouds. Her head feels like a stone. She gets it. Someone should still be growing. It doesn't seem fair. Before going home, they stop for a late diner lunch. Faded yellow counters and aprons. Sliced pies turning in lazy orbits under glass. Their brown-eyed waitress smiling and tired. She needs more comfortable shoes, Naomi thinks. She needs a well-timed compliment.

"Your eyes are really beautiful," she says, her voice a little breathier than intended.

The waitress, to her credit, laughs.

"I got them from the Rent-A-Center." And she shows her crooked teeth. "My pink ones are for the weekend."

Naomi and her father each order coffee and a BLT.

"Shhh,"—a glob of mayonnaise rides the chewing corner of his grin—"Don't tell your mother."

THE HOUSE HASN'T CHANGED SINCE SHE WAS LAST HOME IN August. Same dried hydrangea blooms in a blue bottle in the dining room. Same sprawl of magazines on the living room coffee table. Same river stone paperweight on the entryway desk. The house hasn't changed since she was twelve years old. Naomi heads straight to her old room—to dump her bag, to chew a piece of gum to cover the bacon scent of her breath—while her dad settles into his chair in the living room, begins systematically disassembling a newspaper. On her way through to the kitchen, she offers him a stick of blue wintermint but he shakes his head and grins, holds up a mug full of coffee that was clearly poured this morning. Naomi shrugs and heads into the kitchen where, by the sink, the naked body of a headless turkey tries desperately to escape her mother's slick grasp. Without speaking, Naomi rushes to her side, takes hold of the unwieldy bird and together they wrestle it into a plastic sack, drown it in brine, knot the bag shut and set it in a bowl in the fridge.

"It looks kind of peaceful in there now," Naomi says, almost whispers.

"Slippery little sucker." Her mother closes the door with her hip. Only then do they hug, squeezing one another with elbows, bird-wet hands held safely away. If not for the silver streak in her mother's hair, each would be the perfect reflection of the other.

"Are you glad to be home?" her mother asks into the hair behind her ear.

"I am now," and is surprised to find she means it. "Nothing says 'welcome' like grappling with a dead bird."

Backing out of the embrace: "I hope for your sake," she says, "you're talking about the turkey."

And in response, Naomi deadpans: it's her favorite kind of joke.

They prepare a stuffing of day-old rye and crushed almonds, sautéed vegetables and wine-plump raisins. Then a cranberry nut salad. Then a pot of sweet orange tea to share while outside, a cat winds among the alleyway garbage cans, meowing and sniffing and searching for something unknown even to itself, crying its reports through the air into the open kitchen window. They listen to what little it has to say.

"Sounds like it's got a lot on its mind," Naomi says, "given it only knows one word."

Setting down her tea, her mother points toward the open window, her extended finger like an ordinance in the air.

"One thing," she corrects her. "It's got one thing on its mind."

But neither says what the one thing might be.

Later, passing through the living room, Naomi finds her father happily snoring in his chair, buried in a snow-drift of newsprint.

In the hallway outside her room, the late afternoon sunlight angles in through a window, ignites the polished hardwood floor in a brilliant sheen of white. In this one spot, Naomi cannot see wood grain or seam, the depression of a nailhead, anything. It's like the opposite of a void, not a hole descending through an empty well but an opening, an unlocked door. She stares at the light and wonders what must lie on its other side. She steps over the bright patch and into her room. What was once her brother's room.

THE SCENT OF DUST AND SUN. OF CRAYON AND PAPER AND, faintly, peanut butter. A choreography of toy soldiers in one corner of the room. The closet full of too-small clothes. Neat stacks of notebooks and wild drawings on the wall. Everything arranged at four-feet or under. As if eye-level is at her navel.

Everything but the constellations spraying across the ceiling in glow-in-the-dark flares. The Aleph. The Maccabees. The ladder at the foot of which Jacob sleeps. Constellations of her brother's invention.

Warm and empty, the too-small bed welcomes her like a prayer. Lay me in peace, she thinks, feeling the wings of her scapulas sink into Joshua's mattress indentation. Spread me in shelter like smooth peanut butter. Warm and empty, she sleeps for the first time in two days.

BUT AN HOUR LATER, HER FRIEND KAREN SHOWS UP, PARKS OUT front and leans on the horn, and shouting rushed goodbye-I'll-be-home-for-dinners over her shoulder—her mother still in the kitchen, her father a snoring heap in his chair—Naomi gallops down the stairs, into the chill air of the street and into her friend's waiting car.

"You cut your hair."

"You can stop honking the horn now."

Karen lays off the horn, puts her used Civic in drive, sets them drifting through town. Wind through the open window stirs her mess of long blonde curls. She lights a Newport 100 with a pink lighter shaped like kissy lips. If nothing else, Naomi decides, college has made Karen more essentially Karen. Her sunglass lenses are in the shape of pink stars. Theirs is a soundtrack of laughing chatter (Naomi, as usual, mostly playing the straight man) as Karen aimlessly navigates the town's tree-lined streets, but their words never quite register as memory. It's a fun game, Naomi thinks, this compounding of jokes and innuendo, the plays on words and plays on the past. But it's meaningless. The object of having friends is not the pursuit of meaning but an escape from it. No one seeks a doctorate in companionship. Everyone comes together for a drink after class. Something empty that feels good. Meaningless, but not without purpose.

Eventually, they pull in to a dairy bar near their old high school, set back from the road by a long lawn and bordered behind by the shoals of a dammed creek. Despite the lateness of the season, it's open. High school kids wrapped tight in jackets, fists plunged in their pockets and all lined up for ice cream. Naomi and Karen order a black raspberry milkshake and take their tall styrofoam cup to a picnic table near the water's edge. On the waylaid creek's far shore, a pair of swans patrols the bank-side bulrush and reeds. Naomi sips and watches their oddly draconian movements along the surface. It does not—and in fact never has—occurred to her that this is the same creek her brother once played alongside. The same creek she and her friends, in their own way, would play alongside. Wide and shallow here before tumbling down a short, pointless weir. She sips on her straw and watches the swans' glamour and glide. She wonders what she has that she can throw into the breach.

On her side of the table, Karen whips off her star-shaped sunglasses then snaps her hands like crab claws in the air. "Gimme gimme gimme." Across her oversized grey sweatshirt's breast, in pink academic letters, runs the word PUSSY.

Naomi slides the milkshake across the table's sticky face. In the grass nearby, little birds are chirping and fighting. She expires a jaw-cracking yawn.

"You'll want to get a little sleep before tonight," Karen says, admonishing her with the purple crenulated and dripping end of the straw. "You're going to need it."

But Naomi shakes her head. "No sleep. None for me, thank you."

Licking clean the straw's end, Karen then jams it back through the lid, draws a loud and exaggerated slurp. She does this for a long time. "Burning the candle at both ends, are we?"

"Uh-uh." And she holds up both her hands. "Two candles. I'm burning them both at once."

"Some antibiotics should clear that right up."

In the road running in front of the dairy bar, a pickup roars by, blasting Metallica. A kid in line cups his hands around his mouth and hollers "Kill 'em all!"

"The progressive ideals of the positive youth," Naomi drawls.

"Dude'll be daytrading in five years."

Taking turns sipping long off the shake, they talk for a while about school—Karen attending a state college in the sticks west of here, studying business while surrounded by art students and engineers—about how weird it is to be back home, about how it never gets any less weird.

"They're building a new wing to the high school, did you see?"

"I haven't, no." She can't even picture how their old school used to be. "I've only been back in town a few hours." It's not a mental image she feels any urgency to conjure.

"It's going to be a new gymnasium. Twice as big as the old one."

"Athletes are taller these days."

"The old gym," Karen says with gravity, "will continue to be a gym."

"You know, it's funny. I met this woman, a waitress at the Modern Diner. And she looked so tired. Like she'd been on her feet for a century. So I thought I'd tell her something nice, try and make her feel a little better. So I told her I liked her eyes. And do you know what she said to me?"

"Can't."

"She said they were loaners. She said she rents pink eyes for the weekend."

"Huh." Karen sucks disinterestedly on her straw. "Did it work?"

"Did what work?"

"Did you make her feel better?"

"I'm not sure I made her feel anything."

Karen shrugs, making the folds of her shirt spell PSY. "You can't please everyone, Sams."

"That," Naomi says, "is the credo of an underachiever." What she means to say is: *but I want to.*

Before leaving, they discuss the plan for the evening. Where and when. Who of consequence will be attending. "Bill Regan couldn't come home this year. And I guess Kim Davis wants out."

"Out, really?"

"Really really."

"What a prude."

"Well. She is going to Liberty."

"Some liberty. At least there's still an even number of us."

"Yeah," and Karen winks, "like you've ever had any problem working in the odds."

They agree: nine o'clock beneath the sycamores, on the corner of Riser and Fifth, and in a moment Karen is gone, her Civic rattling to disappear around the bend, but Naomi lingers on a while in the park alongside the shoals. Across the span, the swans are engaging their fluid maneuvers. Now and then, a dead leaf tumbles over the falls. Standing from the picnic table, Naomi walks to the water's edge and digs into her pockets. A couple rumpled dollars. Her dorm keys. A pen. She weighs her options, then throws her keys through the falls. She cannot remember the spoken part, the part that Joshua loved: was the operative word "redeem" or "repent"? It doesn't matter. What's important is the letting go. "Wake up," she whispers. She can always get more keys. "Wake up and return." She watches the water sheer off over the falls, then claps her hands and heads home.

ONE. IF IT DOES NOT HURT ME TO HELP SOMEONE, I WILL help someone.

Two. Sometimes a little hurt is okay.

Three. I will not always say yes. I won't always say no either. But I'll say yes more than I'll say no.

Four. The objective is to be present. But sometimes that means being empty. Now and then, to be present requires being gone.

Five. If I decide something is a problem, I'll decide the solution.

Six. You can live two lives at once.

UNDER NAKED TREE-LIMBS CLACKING. NOVEMBER AIR SHARP in her breath. Not feeling much of anything in these final slow hours of light, Naomi walks the few blocks home. She won't think of it again until much later, but along the way—as scattered handfuls of students mill in the after-school ache of squandered time—she thinks she sees a familiar form. Dark-haired and head down, walking swiftly alone ahead of her. Like he has anywhere to go. Arms full of books and a stray's worried gait. So familiar. But he could be anyone.

She remembers the feel of his hair in her hand. But what she sees are the stars glowing above her bed.

Before turning up her street, she glances his way once more. And maybe he's looking back at her. Or maybe he's already gone.

IN THE HOUR OR SO BEFORE DINNER, SHE TRIES TO STUDY IN HER room, her notebook and text on global health policy open on her bedspread, but her father's frequent passing outside her door—always whistling or humming or clearing his throat—finally forces her to put her books away and join him hip-to-hip on the living room couch to tag-team a crossword puzzle from the paper.

"Keeps the mind sharp like a razor."

"You misspelled 'cufflink.'"

The three of them eat dinner and dessert in the dining room and talk about the common details of their lives away from one another—work and school and the strangers these things give them access to—then all help out cleaning up before playing Scrabble over tea. It's all so wholesome, she thinks, and completely unexceptional. She barely has to try in order to fill her role. It isn't that she doesn't love her parents— she does, and what's more, she likes them. But she wonders if there will ever come a day when they can enjoy one another in all their unique fullness without needing strictly to be together.

When her parents go to bed to read side by side under the glow of their individual bedside lamps, Naomi bides her time—hands folded in her lap, parked on the couch, doing nothing—until she hears her father's snores. She carries her shoes as she creeps out the door. She sneaks out into the night.

Naomi's hair is black and her eyes are near black and her skin is so pale as to almost be blue, though her father insists it's a more Mediterranean complexion: he'll lay one ruddy finger across her forearm for the sake of contrast, then with authority call her "Greenie." It's among the few small victories she grants him. Her default expression is a flat non-smile, giving some people the impression that she's fragile or unfeeling. This impression is immediately forgotten as soon as she speaks or acts. The movement of her mouth the suppression of a smile. A subtle, knowing squint. Her build is slight but athletic: she ran track the last six years of school. In private moments, she thinks of herself as something sleek and nocturnal, a slim hunter unlimited by her size. Not an animal. But not necessarily a person either.

In many ways—her body and dexterity and interest in the social game—Naomi identifies with her mother. In many ways—her understated playfulness, her scholarship, her lack of religious inclination—Naomi identifies with her father. Neither outweighs or is outfavored by the other. She's a piece-by-piece balance of the two. In many ways squared in total divergence from her brother.

Joshua never took school seriously. His intelligence was a toy sword, a magic wand, something to be flourished in play. His young faith was a complicated secret. Everything that wasn't flourished in play was a complicated secret.

The statement often given (when the pressgang demands a statement be given) is that her father wanted an office at home, so Naomi moved into Joshua's room. In one instance—when her dad's partner from the claims office came over for dinner—Naomi volunteered that Joshua's room got better light, which is true though was in no way a motivation. In either case, these became the official stories. A new office. Better light. The truth is that Naomi wanted to make the move, was the instigator, was already spending all of her free time in Joshua's room anyway. Looking through his drawings. Touching his toys, his clothes. Breathing in his fading, lingering scent. Sweat and dust and peanut butter. It was the next logical step in keeping some part of him alive. If only in abstract. If only for herself.

No one has ever asked her why Joshua's belongings still fill the room. If someone did, Naomi's certain: she would not be able to lie. The only change she ever made to the room was to add a small, handmade card to one wall. Colored pencil maple leaves and birch leaves and ash. Autumn red and yellow, autumn purple. She has no idea who made the card.

The room is on the southwest corner of the house. Some afternoons, it's blinding.

When Naomi was almost three and Joshua was just born, she would lie on the floor beside him and stare into his wrinkled sleeping face or into his wide-eyed blinking face. They'd each lie belly-down on the floor and stare, the crowns of their heads pointed in opposite directions, and Naomi would whisper "baby brother." Phonetically: "bebe br're." She'd speak "bebe br're" as a whispered incantation, then later as a playful shout, then simply as his name.

Their mother had gotten pregnant right around Naomi's second birthday. She'd spent nearly half her conscious life to that point waiting for her baby brother to come home. She loved and missed him before there was anything to miss.

It wasn't long after Joshua's death that Naomi began long-distance running. First on her own. Later competitively. She's never considered this a form of escapism, a means to literally run away. She ran to reduce herself to a moving body, a steady breathing working machine cleared of feelings or thoughts. It made her essential. An act of control that was also the opposite of control. By dissolving away her dictated projections, she made herself open to what was already there. It was in this way that she realized her grief was not an obstacle to overcome but an appendage—a hand, a whole arm—that she must learn to use. Her grief was a part of her, was permanent. It didn't have to hurt. It might even be a tool. It was in this way that she came to realize that her brother's death was an act of faulty policy, not of fate. She ran before tests. She ran before writing term papers or breaking up with boys.

The choice to abandon pre-med for global health policy was a similarly found conclusion. Reduced bureaucracy could have saved her brother. Reduced bureaucracy could save thousands in Africa. Some people need more help than others.

More and more over the years, especially since leaving home, Naomi finds that elements of her brother—the details that diverged them, that set them apart—have begun quietly seeping into the warp and weft of her life. A greater willingness and patience for humoring strangers. A gathering disinterest in anything that wasn't continuous or contiguous with the exploration of her work ("play with" always superseding "invest in"). A sudden preoccupation with, if not the faith, at least the rituals of her inherited religion: like sex or a silly movie, it feels good without needing to mean a thing. It's almost as if, stripped of the daily sanctuary of Joshua's room—his drawings and clothes and mostly-gone scent, the lingering dent his body made in his bed—she must now more consciously experience the world for herself and for Joshua as well. To acknowledge his interpretations running alongside her own. To make good on opportunities that only he would have found opportune. The ancient music tingling the Hillel House air each Shabbat. The fragrant crush of herbs between her palms. It's as if now and then, they are both at the same time watching the unspooling world through her eyes. She can feel him sometimes in her fingers, riding on the breath in her lungs. Not the whole of him. Just a part. She wonders how long this feeling will last. In most ways, she hopes it always will.

For the time being, Naomi does not have a boyfriend. Off and on she has, but in recent years there've been no steady partners. At one point in high school, while spending time with one particular boy, she realized how little of herself she was able to give. This boy seemed like an open door to her—all access given without labor or restraint— and also like a puppy, a kitten, some small animal needing to touch and be touched. She found herself to be neither of these things. She could play with, but she could not invest herself in. There was no way she could fulfill this person—any person—amid the total array of duties that comes with being in love. It wasn't fair to either party. Despite what she wanted to be, Naomi knew she was something else. She broke it off with the boy. Now, occasionally, she only has sex. Often with strangers. Men and women. People who seem healthy and vital and safe. Something empty that feels good. Meaningless, but not without purpose. There's always a barrier between them.

It's not long after nine when Karen finds Naomi. A gentle breeze rattles among the trees and errant dead leaves. Air pungent with wood smoke and the underlying funk of half-forgotten Halloween pumpkins, spotted black and slumping with frost-rot on the occasional porch or stoop. It's somehow warmer now at night than it was any point in the day. She makes herself empty to make herself present. Naomi stands beneath a spike-crowned sycamore at Riser and Fifth and waits for Karen to materialize from the dark, take Naomi by the arm, laughingly lead her through the night.

The house on Riser Avenue is boldly alight, a small boisterous sun burning behind its casement windows and clapboard walls. Music seeps muted into the night, a pillow held over a screaming mouth in contrast to the sharp clear voices of the kids on the porch, laughing, joking, smoking and clinking bottles. Naomi leaves Karen outside with the folks gathered there, some of whom she recognizes, all of whom she should know but doesn't. Inside, the music resolves itself into one of the more bouncy songs by The Breeders. There are girls playing games with cups at the kitchen table and boys gossiping by the sink. Couples talking lowly on the stairs. Couples touching unabashed on the couches, in the corners. Some tie-dyes getting high and talking intensely about something dumb. Naomi can't believe she's here. Amid such teenage predictability, it's hard to remember why she is.

Finally, she sees someone she knows, a boy named Seth—curly blonde hair, lean but handsomely fleshy in the face—and in the easy, comfortable way he hugs her hello—not just a greeting but enveloping her in welcome—she realizes: this is probably his house.

"Jesus, Naomi, I'm glad you're here." Seth's holding a red plastic cup in his gesturing hand. "You look great."

"Oh, thank you Seth." From sixth grade on, she and Seth were in every math class together. "You're looking healthy yourself." Oftentimes, they were study partners. "Thanks for hosting tonight." His mouth always tastes like clean water.

"Hey, I'm just glad to finally have the opportunity." He offers to get her a drink, and when he comes back, he leans in close so only she can hear. "Don't worry. It won't be like this for long." And he winks. "My brother's a cop."

She lowers the bottle from her mouth and smiles. "He better be." And when he smiles back, she wonders why mouths are shaped to do the things they do. To bite and snarl but also smile and pray. Is this the optimal tool to conduct so many things? Is this the best we have? Together, Naomi and Seth wade through the bodies to the cool and quiet outside.

WE HAVE MANY REASONS FOR BEING HERE TONIGHT.

Some of us came out of a sincere affection and nostalgia for our friends from only one or two or three years past. We want to gape in surprise at the sight of one another and hug and ask, "How are you?" We want to know everything that's happened, good and bad both, since the last time we got together like this. Want to emphatically agree that we should do this sort of thing more often.

Unless you're Daniel Alotta. In which case, you came ostensibly for these reasons but in fact want—in ways that seem subtle only to you—to gloat over your own accomplishments. Dean's list at Harvard. Full ride. That awesome red Grand Prix parked a safe distance from the other cars, though not so far as to not easily be admired. You will sneer and talk down to people all evening because you're too good to make legitimate friends with any of us. You will not be here to see the evening through.

Whatever. Forget you. We are not you. We are here because we love one another. We're here because we miss the old days. We're here because we miss each other and who we once were, miss who we've each become without each other's company. Tanya Hollings and Jared Weiland got together for a few months in their junior year, then split up out of mutual boredom. Now they secretly watch one another from across the room, from opposite ends of a beer-pong table, amazed at how fascinating the other's become. Her debate-club calm and aplomb have resolved into a quick wit, into keen observation. His benchwarmer politesse has matured into a good-natured, perpetual ease. After the cops come, they'll end up walking away half-drunk together, to get a coffee and split a slice of coconut cream pie at the all-night diner, to eventually find a night's home in Jared's boyhood bed. But these two, also, won't be here to see the evening through.

Some of us have come because we want a second chance. Todd Fisk held a flame for Karen, Naomi's friend, since eighth grade. Nothing ever came of it. He's hoping he might rouse her interest tonight. He's cooler now, he thinks, more confident and more interesting to talk to. He's studying English at Syracuse. He is not, in fact, very confident at all. Nothing will come of his advances tonight because the advances won't ever come. Todd will not see this evening through. Karen, of course, will.

Very few of us will see this party's end. Not the tie-dyes who came just to get high and hear themselves talk. Not the geeky kids who still come to get laid and still don't dare ask for a single beer, let alone speak to a girl—although Carter Hall, short and scrawny-looking though in fact finely muscled upon inspection, will see this night's bright end. But the kids who think they're hot shit won't. And the kids who think they're pieces of shit won't either. Almost no one will be here by the end of the night. The party is a beard to cover the true party. We are our own disguise.

Moments before the police arrive, Naomi and Seth are seated on the edge of a bed in an upstairs room, surrounded by kids playing games. First it's a round of some lame drinking game someone's brought back from her sorority, involving a deck of cards and too many arbitrary rules. Then Hungry Hungry Hippos. Then Don't Break the Ice. A closet in the hallway is loaded with board games. Naomi and Seth sometimes join in, sometimes watch. A game of Parcheesi makes it less than one round before it's abandoned. No one understands how to play Mouse Trap, but it's fun to set up. Eventually, someone brings out a Ouija board and nearly everyone wants to play.

Seth drops down to the floor on his knees, hands poised to barely touch the planchette. Naomi remains on the bed.

"Ah c'mon, Naomi," someone shouts. "Come join us."

"No thank you."

"Why not?" It's Lynn Stevens. Who once punched Naomi in the tit when Naomi cut into a sprint to win a state meet, leaving Lynn second for the team but sixth overall. Lynn will not be here to see this evening through. "It'll be fun."

"Because," she says with practiced calm, "my baby brother died of encephalitis." As if reporting on the weather. "I'd rather not talk to him with all you assholes around."

The response is a mix of laughter and blank stares. But mostly what she reads is unease. Not every joke can land, she thinks. Blame the deadpan delivery. Blame the joke for not being a joke. Naomi rises from the bed and heads downstairs. She's ready for another drink. Along the way, she passes Karen in the hall, pressed against and making out with some boy that Naomi doesn't know. When they see one another, Karen frees her mouth long enough to whisper "practice" with a grin.

With so many people hanging out on the steps—blathering, cackling—she has to creep to get down the stairs, pressing between bodies, struggling to get through. And more than anything, right now, she wants to run. To feel her lungs burn and her mind go blank. To reduce herself down to zero. It was foolish to mention Joshua here, she thinks, foolish to name his death in the presence of a Ouija board. Like he wasn't already all around.

Downstairs, the party has reached a dizzy new height in underage absurdity. Voices are louder and much less coherent, some of the girls having achieved the shrill level of drunk near the edge of violence or tears. Mostly, the guys just laugh. In the kitchen, one girl dances slowly by herself on top of the island counter while nearby a boy nurses a bloody nose and gazes on in awe. It's not even eleven o'clock. It's so totally appropriate when a police officer in motorcycle helmet and leathers manifests among them.

It's a while before anyone takes notice. Mostly, he just stands, calm and observing amid the too-young drunken fervor. When someone finally turns off the music, the cop gives a leather-gloved thumbs-up. The girl on the counter keeps dancing. Without being told to, most people file out, the majority knowing enough to leave their drinks behind. For the rest, a second officer by the door collects their bottles and cups and cans. The cop in the kitchen smiles and says goodnight to the bodies draining into the night, finally helps the dancing girl down from the island, points his chin toward the door and she's gone.

When he sees Naomi, she simply nods. He leaves her be while herding the remaining kids outside.

In the end, only eight people remain. At the door, Seth shakes hands with his brother.

Smiling, incredulous: "You're the only guy I know who'd throw a party and invite the police to break it up."

Seth shrugs. "I like social gatherings. Too many people and it becomes a fucking zoo."

The other cop—somewhere outside, patrolling the dark—is gone.

"Just get the place cleaned up before Mom and Dad get home."

The officer leaves. The air lightens. Or maybe it ignites. Moments later, those who remain reconvene upstairs in Seth's attic bedroom. White Christmas lights strung from the rafters. A couple couches. Cushions piled in various arrangements and a Turkish water pipe at the center of the room. Seth puts on some music—that sad, keyboard-heavy record to which everyone's breaking up with their boyfriends these days—and they gather around, get high, smoke hash mixed with sticky foreign tobacco redolent of fruit and spice.

Karen is the first, standing and announcing she's just high enough, thank you very much. She delivers herself to one of the couches, sinks into the warm soft cushions, closes her eyes and arranges herself into an expression and posture of open invitation. Carter Hall and Michael Talons, the smartly-dressed brown kid, rise and join her, one on either side of the couch, Karen purringly between the two.

Naomi and Seth smoke another round, then sprawl out on a mountain of cushions opposite Karen and the boys. They lie back and watch, grinning, as the three talk and touch, watching as something slowly begins. Around the water pipe, the remaining three kids—Timothy Buck, Sonja Romanchuk, Trisha Kiley—smoke and blather, Tim red-headed and grinning madly, perpetually exuberant, Sonja's accent occasionally rising above the music, Trisha only ever seeming to laugh. It's a beautiful scene, Naomi thinks. Our holiday of gratitude. Zero out and let go.

Leaning in close to Seth, she asks, "Is that Nigra kid still around, do you know?"

Silhouetted on the street. Clutching tight his books.

"Who, Ben?" Seth looks away from the show on the couch. "Mr. Roboto? Yeah, I think he's still around. Still in high school, I think. Why?"

She's suddenly very conscious of the comfort in her body. The cushions beneath her back and Seth nestled along her side. The smoke in the air tickles her nose. She's high.

"We should invite him next time." She watches Karen's hands—one in either lap—sliding over and squeezing the thighs in her grasp. "We should have invited him from the get-go."

"Seriously? Why?" Head propped up on an elbow, Seth's free hand rests lightly on her belly. "I didn't know you guys even knew one another."

For the first time all night, she legitimately wants to

laugh: how can anyone ever know someone else?

"He used to be friends with my brother." Small and serious about everything. The games he'd play with Joshua always like research. Like something might be revealed if their play was conducted correctly. "Way back when." Then later, just a shadow around town until his freshman year, suddenly there and present in her homeroom. "We actually had a thing for a little while." Getting high on the tracks near the creek. Making out in the tall grass. Finally sneaking him into her room, into her bed, together sharing their bodies in her brother's old room. "But that was a long time ago." Lying beside one another and staring at the constellations glued to the ceiling. "Mostly we just talked about my brother." Constellations Joshua had glued to the ceiling.

"Your brother." Across from them, Karen is kissing Michael's mouth while Carter Hall kisses Karen's neck. The boys' pants are undone. She's got a cock in each hand. There are much fewer clothes on around the water pipe. Seth places his head on Naomi's belly. "Baby brother."

"Baby brother." Her words hum through her body into Seth's ear. She's almost ready. But not yet.

"There are some things about him I forget that I know." Her voice is a breathless whisper. "Then I remember and it's like: how could I forget that?" She sees the water pouring off the dam. "So eager to let go." She sees her keys falling in. "How could I forget?" Forgetting your fingers. Forgetting the length of your body.

"Are you talking about that Ben kid or your brother?"

Seth's voice hums through her belly. That tickles, too.

But she doesn't answer. Wake up and let go. His hands trace the geography of her hips. Her fingers lace through his hair. Let go. Seth helps her out of her pants.

What is that sound beneath the music and their breathing? Beneath the rushing blood in their ears, the sudden surprise of laughter? The muscles and sweat and spit-slick lips? They wrestle for a while, pulling at clothes and at each other, and finally he's over her and finally he's inside her and she closes her eyes, writhing and quivering and finally somehow—somehow—free, no longer anyone or anything—the negative space that her shadow once inhabited, an absence in the shape of her body—and when she opens her eyes, it's not Seth above her but someone else—Michael, dusky and friendly-eyed—but it doesn't matter. How can a face or name ever matter? She turns around for him and arches her back, then turns again to peel off his condom and swallow him and already, there's someone else behind her, a hand and then a mouth, probably Karen or Sonja's mouth and it doesn't matter. She's awake. Michael leaves and someone else takes his place, someone else in her mouth, and it doesn't matter. A mass of arms and legs writhes on the bed while Seth and Karen, naked, kneeling, laugh and pass the water pipe. Naomi closes her eyes and surrenders herself to whatever is going to happen, embraces whatever is already happening because this is what she wants. More than anything else. To serve a purpose that's necessary but is also play. Like running. All of them together running. Burning with each other so close to zero, rarefied and essential, as above them the Christmas lights evenly shine: constellations on a string.

She remembers—vividly remembers, even though she was only three—lying on the floor with her nose nearly touching his nose, on her belly and staring at his squeezed-shut eyes, his upside-down wrinkled raisin newborn face. She remembers the wet sound of his breath and saying his name over and over again—"baby brother, baby brother"—as if that was her entire world. The sound of his name. The landscape of his sleeping face. As far as she can recall, this is her earliest memory. Until there was Joshua, the world did not exist. The full rack of null-sets before the stopwatch starts its tally. This is where the world begins.

It's just past three a.m. when they disband from Seth's house. The boys seem mostly happily exhausted as they head to their separate cars. Sonja and Trisha leave together, still holding hands. Naomi and Karen hug for a moment under a linden before parting, make plans to call one another the following afternoon. From the dark, Carter Hall offers them a ride home. Karen accepts, but Naomi only smiles and waves, says nothing, begins slowly walking up the hill.

There's still plenty of time. She could hang out. Have breakfast at the all-night diner. Go back to someone's house for a drink. Stay the night with Seth under his strings of soft white light. But the streets are empty and silent as a prayer. No leaves to rustle. No birds to sing. The lightest of breezes stirs a candy wrapper along the street, its skittering on the pavement an animal sort of sound. This whole town is a graveyard and this whole town is hers. She walks slow and deliberate through her sleeping streets.

And of course, this becomes an exercise. A game of memory. Each street corner and alcove, each missing brick in the masoned sidewalk corresponds to a particular event. A certain summer drive with Karen through town, music loud, going nowhere, nothing spectacular or even unique but somehow perfect in its timing and execution, the platonic ideal of two friends and a wide open August night. Making out with a boy from another school in the darkened doorway of the Russian Orthodox Church while organ music thrummed through timbers and stones into the marrowed heart of their bones. Falling out of the copper beech by the ball field when she was twelve, startled and excited by it—the sudden wind, the greeting earth— excited even when she realized she'd snapped her wrist. Racing her brother to the dairy bar by the dam, deliber- ately letting him win so she could follow him, running two steps behind to watch him, make sure nothing happened, make sure he was okay, and then later, barely tasted, they threw their cones triumphantly into the dam. As her path leads her out of the town square and up a steep hill, she wonders how closely our memories are tied to the physical topography of the world. That maybe the landscape doesn't simply trigger something within us. That maybe our mem- ories are impressed into the world, are part of the qualities of every possible thing. Like the sound of a voice becoming a record's vinyl groove. The voice is gone. But its imprint remains. Perhaps the experience of falling from a tree and breaking your wrist is a characteristic of the tree, as much a part of it as its particular leaves and particular bark. The memory belongs to the tree. It shares it with you when you're together.

Climbing the hill, Naomi listens as a church bell somewhere tolls four o'clock. She knows her theory doesn't work. Some memories are a constant. Some follow like a dog at your heels. As she reaches the cemetery—walks alongside its stone and iron wall and pushes through the gate—she decides that maybe it's not universally true. Maybe only some memories become the world's and not your own. Because there's only so much room in any person's head. Because there are some things she remembers only when she's finally come home.

Joshua's grave is high up on the hillside, set off and away from most of the other stones, buried alongside the handful of other Jews who've lived and died in this tiny town. A low fence and gate separates these graves from the rest: a nation contained within a nation. Nearby, a tall horse chestnut stands guardian, massive but inviting with its densely interlocking crown. In the spring, Naomi knows, there'll be white flowers. But right now, there's only a framework of black against the sky. Gazing past the chestnut's limbs, she sees the shape of Aleph among the stars. She spots Jacob's ladder ascending. She forgets these constellations aren't real. Settling down in the frosty grass, Naomi leans her back against her brother's simple grave—just a name and a date and a Star of David—and quietly talks with Joshua as they watch the eastern sky slowly brighten over their town, their home—tells him of the people she's met and the things she's felt, the details of a life lived for two—and as dawn melts like a spill of honey over the white-rimmed edge of the world, Naomi has to admit, this too has been a day worth living.

Awake, O You Sleepers
5756 & 5757

O MY CHILD, SO CLEVER AND WISE, YOUR FATHER HAS BROUGHT home a cat. He says it's too quiet here now since (such a curious way of putting it) you kids are both gone your separate ways. But the cat he came through the door cradled close to his chest with one arm doesn't seem too terribly noisy to me. He brought her in and set her down in the kitchen where I was sipping a cup of tea and doing a crossword (correcting your father's mistakes), and she immediately trotted down the hall and plopped in the sunlight splashing on the floor. Her fluffy black-and-orange tummy rising and falling with such gorgeous rigor with each breath. Eyes all but squeezed shut. What an enviable trait, being able to adapt so quickly and joyfully and not the least bit concerned as to what she's adapting to. I'm certain, she was purring.

He didn't say where the cat is from. But I suspect she's

the one that's been living in our alley. Singing up to our window whatever gems she's found in our trash. The splendor of a tuna can. The luxury of a fatty brisket strip. A grateful creature. Inside, she doesn't sing anymore. Only vibrates with pleasure as she pads around our home, window-light gleaming off her coat of many colors.

It's like it's slipping our minds, the way neither one of us has given her a name.

Nisan 14, 5756

In the dream, all four of us go together down to the green space by the shallows. The sky is thick with a gauze of fog lying heavily everywhere, but the grass greens up like nothing I've ever seen. Grass from some other world.

I can hear but cannot see birds: starlings, unpredictable and squealing like hinges. Your father is carrying a picnic basket. Every time I look at him, he's eating something else. This part could easily not be a dream. I leave your father parked on his haunches on the grass

Down near where the glassy water calmly lips the shore, I find you two kids and you're standing side by side. You're wearing matching blue and white shirts. Something geometric. When you see me, you both cock your heads to the side and point to some vague thing to your left and behind you. It's like this perfect choreography, how you do this together, in the same way, at the same time. Then you both turn and run toward wherever you've pointed in the fog, and I realize it is not so much a choreography as a mirror. You are each the other's reflection. Which makes you the same person. I watch my children as one person disappear into the fog, and when I turn away to look at your father, he's eating a meat pie. Little curls of steam fold like fleur-de-lis up from where he's busted the crust. He raises his fork in a little salute, then says something in Hebrew about the world to come. But I cannot understand a word he says, for his stupid mouth is full.

Nisan 15, 5756

OUR INSTRUCTIONS TODAY ARE TO TELL THE CHILDREN, BUT there really isn't a whole lot to tell. The bread has been burned and the fruit has been crushed. Herbs laid out purposefully with oil on the table. And there is wine. But there is no father. Where is your father? Your father is bowling. Your father is an idiot.

Iyar 12, 5756

YESTERDAY WAS SUCH A GORGEOUS DAY AND AFTER SUCH A LONG ugly winter, it was more like compulsion than choice how I went down to the Agway in town and wandered dumbstruck through their greenhouse, just about drunk on the hot scent of new leaves and coming home with an armload of flowers. Viola and petunia and a trailing sash of portulaca. Some other things whose names I can't remember. Nicotiana. I brought them home and planted them in the two big urns in the backyard, the ones on either side of the door leading up the back stairwell. They looked so nice there, all lush living colors against the black metal of the urns and the wet black potting soil and the wispy blue sky, all composed as a striking postcard commemorating the promising season to come. Things will be better this year. What else can a picture like this say? But when I went outside this morning, the grass in the yard was all covered in frost and my new plants in their urns were dead. Withered black like too old spinach forgotten in the fridge. Your mother is no gardener, kiddo. I can't even really fake it. Your grandfather would be ashamed. You'd think I'd be used to this by now, would have given up or anyway, not take it so hard. But it makes something in me go cold each time, to know these things, so fragile and vulnerable, depend on me for life, and I fail them.

Your father even told me we'd get a frost in the night. I could have covered them with a towel and saved them. The obvious profundity of prevention being the best cure. Why didn't I listen?

Sivan 6, 5756

YOUR FATHER LEFT FOR WORK AND I GATHERED UP AND reassembled the sloppy anarchy of his morning paper, bound it with a rubber band and set it on the table next to his chair in the living room. Then I walked into town for some pie. When I came home, the paper was undone and on the floor and in a mess. Like someone had tried to make a papier-mâché castle on a frame of nothing and without the mâché. The cat was asleep in the hallway. Stretched out on her back to let the morning sun warm her belly of ten million colors. Not exactly the portrait of guilt. I asked her anyway if she did it, and she summarily dismissed the charge by responding not at all.

So who did it?

Sivan 24, 5756

YOUR FATHER'S DUG OUT HIS TELESCOPE FROM THE CRAWLSPACE above the hall. He hasn't had it out in years. I wonder what made him think of it now. I can remember the two of you out in the backyard almost every night the summer he first brought it home, looking at whatever the hell you each saw up there. But that was a long time ago. Yet here he is now, out in the backyard, peeping through his little viewfinder while I finish up the dishes all alone.

What does he see up there? What did you see together?

Sivan 27, 5756

PASSOVER YOUR FATHER FORGETS BUT FLAG DAY? FLAG DAY, he remembers. He's out there in the backyard now, flapping a flag around like a moron. If the wind turned and the flag tried to choke him, I swear, I do not think I'd help save his life.

Tammuz 6, 5756

I HAVE A NEW STUDENT. THE YOUNGEST BABOON IN THE GARRITY family. Ten lessons, once a week through the summer. In the school's music room in the afternoon dusk, she looked so small and scared, like a little lost girl in the forest, singing to keep herself company, singing to keep less afraid. Even with her stud-pierced bottom lip. Even with her black T-shirt and the word ZERO silkscreened across her breasts. A lost girl hunted by wolves in the woods. But then she said she wanted to learn how to sing that Smashing Pumpkins' song, that awful fake opera thing that's always playing on the radio now, and she even demonstrated, making her nose buzz like a cicada. It was like the panicked repeating tone you used to get if your dialed a disconnected number, how that tone sounded through an old rotary phone. Only she had less rhythm than that. I explained to her that there are some ways of singing you can't learn, you can only discover. Billy Corgan sings the way he sings through discovery. There was no one to teach him what he knows. (She seemed surprised that I knew the singer's name. Maybe that earned me some points?) It was as kind a way as I could figure to deliver to her this news. You really can't be any damn thing you dream up. I'll never be a famous phlebotomist. Your father will never be a prima ballerina. And young Meghan Garrity will never be a dead-ringer for the whinging Billy Corgan. To her credit, she seemed to take it well. She said she'd settle for Tori Amos. We spent our lesson learning what notes were.

Tammuz 9, 5756

I could watch the cat for hours. In fact, I do. She's a genius at doing precisely nothing.

Tammuz 17, 5756

Well, here's yet another remarkable entry in my

ongoing chronicle of neglect. For years I've been keeping a little herb garden in the window box in the kitchen. Thyme and summer savory and oregano. I'm always surprised when they come back each spring. But they do. They always do. Just last week, they looked so good, bursting with fresh green and trailing over the box's edge. But today when I checked, they looked funny and dried up, and when I opened the window and touched them, they just rolled around on top of the dirt. Their roots were all gone. Just the tops like tumbleweeds. Like they weren't even sure for themselves yet that they were dead. Which struck me as the most pathetic part of all. The oregano was still pushing brand new tiny leaves. Tender and green and unquestionably dead.

What am I doing wrong? Why am I still doing this wrong?

Tammuz 26, 5756

YOUR FATHER IS AN IDIOT.

Tammuz 29, 5756

DEAREST WEIRDO,

Yesterday, I drove to the hair salon and then drove to the grocery store for some potatoes and milk, and then I just drove. Out of town and up and down these hills that some glacier chiseled into the earth a billion years or more ago, and I had all the windows rolled down so now my haircut was already a mess but it felt so fine, kiddo, I didn't care. There are eagles in the air and worms in the dirt. It's funny how much I miss your father when he's the only one who's still around. I stopped and had lunch at some little roadside sandwich shop at the crossroads of two county highways that hadn't even earned the credence of a flashing yellow light, then I headed back for home. I felt like having a beer. How often do I ever want a beer? I was celebrating the simple wonder of this great big hurtling world and the fact that I get to live in it—I get to drive around and eat sandwiches and have my hair cut in a salon that smells like coconut shampoo—and acknowledging that I was living was the celebration. Prayer by means of doing. Who wouldn't want a beer? But I was setting myself up. Just as I was getting into town, I came to a stop sign, and in that one single second I was stopped, a downy white feather blew through the car. In through the passenger side and over the console to turn one graceful summersault before my nose, then drifting on out the driver's side window. I watched it float through, half in awe and half amused. Then I started bawling. Your mother can be such a fool. I guess it all has to do with scale. This tiny fragile thing versus the crushing enormity of the world that is, somehow dancing when it ought to be ground meanly into nothing. A delicate white puff. Turning summersaults. The driver behind me blatted his horn and I had to wave him past. But just doing that, just signaling to a frustrated stranger, was enough to break the spell. My face was wet but I was calm. The feather was gone and maybe never was. I drove home and cooked dinner for your father. Everything was fine. Even still, you'd think I'd be better at this by now.

Av 1, 5756

LAST NIGHT, YOUR FATHER CAME INTO THE KITCHEN TO ASK ME what I was doing.

"Writing a letter," I said.

His eyes got real big behind his glasses. "Oh" was all he said. Then he went back to his paper in the living room, where the cat had stolen his chair.

Av 5, 5756

SURPRISE SURPRISE. MY NEW STUDENT DID NOT SHOW TO HER lesson today. As she has skipped almost all of her lessons so far this summer. Is it harder or easier teaching your class when all your students consistently skip their lessons? I suppose I have an obligation to call her parents and report her absence. Yet somehow, it doesn't seem like any of my business. My dominion extends only to this room and only for one hour. Everything else is beyond my jurisdiction. If the parents don't know where their children go each afternoon, well, then.... But I wonder, do they know that their kids are playing hooky? Another question might be: do the parents know that it's summer vacation? Kids *should* be jigging their summer classes. Goofing off down by the creek and kissing their crushes in the shadows beneath the trees. That said, it'd be nice to have a reason to be hanging around the school all the time.

Whatever. I mean, it's not a total wash. As much time as I spend alone, I really don't mind a little extra quiet solitude. There is a calm, forgotten solemnity to the school music room in the summertime that is lost once fall classes start. There's a casual holiness here. There is also a piano. When a student doesn't show, I spend the hour fingering out tunes, playing songs for the dim secret temple. There's always dust dancing through the sunlight. I keep the overhead lamps turned off. Today I played a much-slowed-down version of "Misirlou" and an old klezmer tune your grandfather taught me but whose name I don't remember. Then I surprised myself by remembering all the words to "Motion Pictures." I played "These Arms of Mine," which is so simple but so good, then played Sam Cooke's version of "The Riddle Song," and as dumb as that song is, I almost missed the last rising notes because something terrible was twisting in my throat, and I was crying. How dumb is that? Why am I always crying now over the most stupid things? Why should I be so moved by floating feathers and songs about cherries and chickens? The folded-up music stands remained unmoved and unimpressed. The dancing dust in the sunlight didn't care. Yet I, I was a mess. I sat there with the piano slowly vibrating its strings into silence and waited and listened, wondering when I became so senti-mental, wondering if the strings ever did stop humming or if they only ever just got too quiet for anyone to actually hear. Can such a thing ever be still, really still? How would you know? I closed the lid on the keys and sang to myself the last line again—*"and a baby when it's sleeping…"*—then stood to lock up for the night.

Av 9, 5756

A WOMAN IN THE GROCERY TODAY STOPPED ME TO SAY THAT I ought to be ashamed of my actions in Palestine. She was holding a melon, which seemed in counterpoint to whatever argument she was trying to make. One cannot wag their political finger while cradling large fruit like it's an infant. I'm certain, that's against the rules. I told her I've never been to Palestine. I explained to her the difference between Israelis and Jews. She didn't seem pleased. I didn't apologize and neither did she. She took her cantaloupe and stomped off.

It's a drag sometimes being marooned here on this desert island of white white white people.

Av 12, 5756

I WENT IN TO THE SCHOOL FOR MY LESSON TODAY AND SAT at the piano to plink out a song in what is now my new usual solitude, and a moment later just about jumped out of my skin when the Garrity girl walked in through the door. As if I had any right to be surprised. Like it wasn't for her lesson that I was there in the first place. I hadn't seen her in weeks. Her hair was now dyed half pink and half blue like a puff of cotton candy. She was wearing a Type O Negative shirt, so on her chest were two women making out. I wonder what it's like for her grandparents, who thirty years ago probably told their own children that they looked crazy and listened to devil music, and now must bear witness to this. Personally, I think it's wonderful. If each new generation cannot shock those previous with a unique and scary unimagined future, then someone isn't doing their job.

I told her I liked her shirt.

The Garrity girl and I talked for a while, me at the piano bench while she slouched in the scoop of a plastic blue chair. I had a lesson plan for the day (I'd been adhering to my original syllabus all these weeks, preparing for each class while perfectly aware that I'd likely deliver the lesson to no one) but of course that didn't make sense anymore. I asked her what songs she was really excited by today, if they were anything I might not know, which she scoffed at but only in an obligatory way (after all, she knows I know who Billy Corgan and Peter Steele are). I asked if she had a portable CD player and if she'd be interested in sharing something with me, and first she made a screwed-up teenager face at me, but then she dug through her backpack and pulled out a discman and a binder of CDs, and I have to admit, I was startled when I slipped on the headphones. The music was heavy (grated fuzz being the ambrosia our youth pine for), but more than that, it was aggressively minimal. It was making a point not to change, or anyway, to not change too much. The singer sounded like he was speaking in a dream. All breath and whisper. It also didn't seem like he knew English very well. Like he was just saying words he liked the sound of. When the song was over, I took off the headphones and played the opening riff on the piano, rolling the chugging chords into an arpeggio, and now the Garrity girl was the one who looked surprised. Clearly it was news to her, the simplicity of power chords, the wide openness of their translation. I played the intro left-handed and looked at the Garrity girl and in a minute, she got it. She sang the opening words. *Hear me spit.* What a horrible, wonderful command! Is there a better way to register a complaint? The sound—not the act—of spitting. We played the whole stupid song. In the staccato breaks, I slapped one hand against the piano's face like a snare drum. It hurt my hand, and I liked that it hurt. In the song's build and final release, we sang the chorus together, and even though the girl's voice was bad—I mean, truly, terribly, leagues from being in key—I did my best to harmonize, hitting the off-sevenths and -fifths to her off-melody. *I get bored!* Like we were pleading with someone who can make the world different. *I get bored!* Like we're missing something vital that neither one of us can name.

Av 20, 5756

Dear Hairlip, Dear Clubfoot, Dear Noodle,

Today I found myself standing outside your bedroom door. Like I had any reason to go in there. Like I had any reason to hesitate. I laid my hand against the wood. But I did not go inside. I have no idea how long I stood there like that.

More and more often, I find myself doing this sort of thing. Like watching the steam swirl up from my teacup through the clear morning light until there's no more steam and my tea is grown cold. That sort of thing. My mind travels a long ways away, and when it comes back, I can't know where it's been. But I can guess. Yesterday, I don't know how long I spent just watching the colored lights from the prism in the window steadily move across the kitchen. (Where I've begun staring and losing track of time, your father has begun more and more buying me these dumb gifts. Like a wooden top with black and white stripes that turns hypnotic when it spins. Or this prism that I hung up in the kitchen. Things you can get entirely lost inside. I guess maybe like his telescope, still set up in the yard. I can imagine him there in whatever store he finds these things, just staring at this or that thing, whatever's caught his awe. I can see him, as if in a trance, bearing with wonder this object or that object up to the waiting cashier, perhaps lost in the very same memory-scrubbing revelry that's been eating up my days. The giving is nice, and these things are not entirely junky. But still. Who does he think he's buying these for? Does he know? Do I?) For whatever reason, yesterday I was drawn to the dot of blue light. Sometimes other colors grab hold of me. But this time, it was the blue. Like a little swimming fish. It seemed somehow more visceral than the other colors. Isn't that dumb? Visceral light. I probably would have watched the colors circle the room until the sun went down if the phone hadn't started ringing. Even that took me a moment to notice. When I answered, it was the mother of that Garrity kid. I'd forgotten to go to our lesson. For once, the tables were turned.

Av 22, 5756

THE CAT'S FAVORITE SPOT IN THE HOUSE IS THE HALLWAY'S end, near the bedrooms, where the afternoon sun falls through the window warm and blinding white. She raises her arms and rolls on her back and is the idealization of perfect tranquility. A sleepy cat lolling in a wash of limitless white. In the exact same spot where you and your idiot friend loved to play.

Elul 1, 5756

DEAREST BACKFLIP,

I got a letter from your sister today. I have written to her three times since she left for Cameroon, but she only wrote in response to the first letter I sent. It takes so long for things to get there, for things to come back. It's not even like a dialogue. Just two people shouting from what might as well be whole other worlds. Each praying that the other can hear. Sometimes I imagine she's with you. The two of you together on the far side of some smoking river, far away but at least not alone. For all the difference it makes, I might as well be shouting across the same exact void.

But that's an ugly attitude to take. It's not a void. It just takes longer to respond. Though to be honest, kiddo, I sometimes feel so foolish writing to you this way. I *know* you cannot hear me, that you're not reading this over my shoulder as I write. But that's how it feels. Like you're right here with me. Whether I want you here or not. I know that isn't how this world works. We've neither one of us yet entered the world to come. But somehow, I cannot stop myself. It's like you're only gone for now and soon, sometime, you'll be back. I don't want you to miss anything while you're away. Even if all you're missing is just your mom missing her kids.

Elul 3, 5756

What I have so far learned about Cameroon:

o Its oldest continuous inhabitants are the Baka People, who are considered pygmies, but I wonder what that even means anymore: pygmy. Despite how long they have been in the region, they are vastly discriminated against. Which honestly doesn't strike me as anything new.

o The first Europeans there were Portuguese sailors. Who knows where they were going. This was decades before Christopher Columbus rammed his *Santa Maria* into the unexpecting flank of the Americas. These Portuguese were astonished by the number of shrimp that populated a particular river, so they named the entire region *Rio dos Camarões*. Shrimp River. The name has stuck for over five hundred years. Which, if nothing else, gives evidence to the importance of first impressions.

o The shrimp, I'm told, are known as Ghost Shrimp. I wonder why.

o All at once, I'm reminded (this has nothing to do with

Cameroon) of those old Head & Shoulders commercials from a thousand years ago. I was about to say they were from before your time, but it occurs to me, sadly, they're from after. Some teeny-dreamy hunk gazing with unmitigated longing at a girl in a swimsuit, her sleek legs extending all the way to the moon, then tossing his head (apparently in a cloud of flaking dander) to dewy-eyed address the camera: "You never get a second chance to make a first impression." Which, of course, is true (TV can, in spite of itself, be truthful when delivering its stupidities). But do you ever get a second chance at anything? Go ask the laundry list of dead herbs and annuals I've killed already this year.

o   Over the centuries, the country has been ruled by Christian missionaries and Muslim slave-traders. No Jews. Also: German, French, and British colonists. Every last one of them eventually lost their claim. They always lost it to war.

o   The diversity of Cameroon's landscape often earns it the title of Little Africa. There are deserts and beaches, mountains and savannas and rainforests in between. And that is where my daughter lives. In the jungle (or so I imagine: her letter was not clear on this point). Passing her days in a place so different from home, it might as well be a different planet. Arguing with administrators and adlibbing clinics from open-air canvas tents. Helping the poorest people she meets. Turning no one away.

o   The government there is considered one of the most

corrupt in the world. Police and soldiers are frequently accused of abusing and torturing minorities, homosexuals, suspected criminals, political activists. These are the people my daughter lives among. This is where she chooses to be. But they've apparently got one hell of a football team.

o   Literacy is high but health is low. Every medical establishment is understaffed, yet there are nurses and doctors who are out of work. There is no money to pay them. Life expectancy is among the lowest in the world. All of this is a policy choice. I think that bears repeating: all of this is a choice. Commonplace epidemics include dengue fever, malaria, meningitis, and sleeping sickness (I'm not sure what that is but it sounds amazing and possibly magical, like something from a fairy tale, though in all likelihood it's not too different from what you caught from a mosquito in the fall of '82). Also: AIDS and HIV (nothing magical there), cases of which go under-reported because of the prevailing social stigma. So boys and girls are spreading disease to maintain their status within their community. Again, if policy changes were taken into effect, all of this could be reversed.

o   Cameroon is one of the richest countries in Africa.

o   Its people are poor and they are dying.

o   My daughter is there among them.

o   There are scarier places in the world. But not for me. Not anymore.

o   It's almost like a song one of my students might prettily
    sing. "There are no Jews in Cameroon."

Elul 8, 5756

AFTER CLEANING THE KITCHEN THIS AFTERNOON, I LAY ON THE
couch to rest for a while, and the cat came up and nestled
in under my chin, and it was so cozy there with her that I
didn't even notice I was asleep. I was on a bus in some city
and I was heading to the botanical gardens. I remember, I
was excited to see all the late azaleas in bloom. I thought
I recognized some of the people on the bus but I couldn't
figure out who they were. But that was okay. I rode the bus
and felt the sunlight splashing warm and white all over
me, and at one stop, you got on and came and sat next
to me. So now we were both in the light. It didn't seem
like you'd planned it, but it also didn't seem like you were
surprised to see me. Like this happened all the time. And
the thing is, I wasn't surprised either. We sat side by side
in the sun's rinsing light and didn't speak, and a few stops
later, you got off. It appeared you were going to the library.
I looked out the window while the bus pulled away. You
waved. I started getting excited again about seeing the
azaleas in bloom.

Elul 11, 5756

TODAY WAS MY LAST LESSON WITH THE GARRITY GIRL. FALL
classes start next week. If this does not signal the sum-

mer's end, I do not know what can. But for that one class in the middle of July, she has skipped every lesson since first arriving here with her dreams of singing in a grunge rock band. I wonder what she's done with her secreted time. Smoked cigarettes? Flirted with the older boys? Maybe let them furtively touch her for the first of many times? I feel like, in some way, I must have failed this girl with her clown hair and black fingernails. Like something more was expected of me, but neither of us knew what, and as a consequence, we both lose. She came and she sang for me her one final time, and it was like we'd never met before. She was awful. But I wonder if maybe that was her point. To not sing pretty. To not sing at all. Only to make a noise with her body that sounded exactly the way she felt.

Here is the moment where I could have connected to this girl. I could have asked her where she's been while skipping on her voice lessons. Asked not as an adult, but as an equal. Two women in a room. I could have asked what she's learned out there on her own. It might have made me feel better about accepting her parents' money. But I didn't ask anything. There is an infinite distance between us, I realized while I played the piano and she meowed like a sick cat. And as I considered this distance, it only grew greater. Like the old riddle about firing arrows at the sun. *The more you shoot, the more you may.* How could we ever reach each other, she and I? How could we ever connect? Is this just me? Or is this everything? Is it the entire world that is withdrawing from itself? By trying to draw nearer, are we pushing it all away? They say the universe is expanding. So let's blame the universe. The empty space between everything just making more empty space. All to no greater purpose than to make that which *is* that much less significant compared to that which *isn't*. We finished playing her awful song, and I told her good job, and she used her feet to make more distance as she walked out the music room's door, and all of it was the universe's fault.

But what if it's not? What if this is like Cameroon? How much could be different is I simply changed my mind? How much closer might I be to everything that's far away, if only I changed my mind?

Later, as I walked out of the school and into the afternoon light, a little dust devil rose up in the parking lot. Spinning for all it's worth. Our entire faith and culture is founded on mistaking such things as signs from God. Am I any better or worse? The column of wind rose taller and gathered up candy wrappers and dust. Then it met the side of a parked station wagon, and tore itself to pieces, and was gone.

Elul 29, 5756

WHAT WOULD YOU HAVE BEEN DOING ON THIS DAY, I WONDER. You would have been at school. You'd be chewing the golden-yellow paint off your stubby number 2 pencil. You'd be multiplying an ever-increasing complexity of numbers. You'd barely be hiding your grin as you waited to raise you hand to terrorize your teacher with some new riddle or contradiction. You'd raise your hand and she would not call on you, because already, she'd have your number. This isn't even conjecture, kid. I've got evidence on you! You'd run home from school and slide in your socks across the hallway floor, into the splashing white light that our cat now loves so much. And there your friend would be with you, too. Like a ghostly little shadow. Somehow answering your questions without either of you having to speak.

What would you be doing now today, I wonder. You'd be going to work. You'd be flirting with the girls. I believe it likely you'd be flirting with the girls. (Even at eight, you were a charmer.) People would laugh even if what you said wasn't a joke. Because even serious things, to you, are a joke. Were a joke. Even serious things were a joke. But now nothing is anything to you anymore.

But it's hard for me to believe that when all I seem to do is talk to you. Write you letters and play with the cat, then write letters about playing with the cat.

I wonder if I'll ever feel as if you aren't always, always around.

Tishri 1, 5757

I NEEDED SOMETHING IN MY POCKET BEFORE I LEFT THE HOUSE, so I took the old dried hydrangea blooms—something you and your dad brought home for me a million years ago— from their blue bottle on the entryway table. I was wearing my long blue peacoat the color of faded forget-me-nots, so the pockets were deep. No one would ever guess I had dead flowers hidden there. I walked through town under an oddly cold sky, expecting from the chill alone to see autumn colors, but everything was vibrant and green. The honeysuckle vines were still blooming pink and orange like little florescent bursts, and the cloudy flowers in the hydrangea bushes had all turned from white to pink. But these blooms, of course, were much younger than those in my pocket. Why had I saved these for so long? What a stupid question. The living flowers threaded a honey scent in the air. I walked through our sleepy afternoon town until I came to the green space overlooking where the creek backs up and pours over the dam. Just a little ways off, some folks were hanging around the dairy bar, licking cones and spooning sundaes into their faces. Who doesn't love a sundae? I stood with my boots sinking in the trucked-in sand along the water's edge and watched the pale cataract of the dam and the fishy ripple of light shining off the creek's face, the swans parading like soldiers among the water lilies and the far bank's reeds. I could tell, the ice cream people were watching me. Let them watch. I tossed the dead flowers into the water. I followed them as they flowed alongside the bank. I watched them tumble over the dam. After that, they were lost to me. In the shoals above the dam, the swans balanced up on their tails and honked madly at me, whacking their wings against the water. So I clapped, too. I clapped and shouted to them, "Awake, O you sleepers, awake from your sleep!" The stark cream and dun of wings splashing, beads of water like chandelier glass sparkling up into the air. They honked and clapped and I clapped and called back. "You slumberers! Awake from your slumber! Search your deeds and turn!" But the swans did not turn in repent. As far as I could tell, they did not search their deeds. I stopped clapping and the birds stopped clapping and I guess that was that. I joined the staring ice cream people at the dairy bar and enjoyed a raspberry shake.

Yet another thing I miss with you being gone, kiddo. No one to celebrate the holidays with.

Tishri 10, 5757

IN THE DARK BESIDE ME, YOUR FATHER SAYS HE'S SORRY. IN THE kitchen there are apples sweetly off-gassing their ethylene perfume. At the foot of the bed, the cat sleeps on our feet. The office that was once a bedroom is silent and the bedroom that's now a museum is silent and beside me in the dark, your father says he's sorry. I tell him he's forgiven already. I tell him, apology accepted. But I know, I will need to tell him all over again before any of this is through.

Tishri 13, 5757

YOUR FATHER BROUGHT ME HOME AN EGG ROLL TODAY. A single warm egg roll. Wrapped in a wax-paper sleeve. What kind of thoughts gas around in that brain of his? I wonder.

Pork egg roll.

Tishri 15, 5757

WHEN YOUR FATHER CAME HOME FROM WORK, HE FOUND ME in the living room, sitting inside a fort of blankets and couch cushions and chairs. I had some magazines inside with me, and some crosswords to finish correcting, and a cup of tea and the cat. She was spread out across my lap like a map of the forgotten world. Nations of orange and black and white and cream. I scratched her belly, and all the lands changed hands.

For a moment, I could hear your father standing in the living room door, knew he was staring at my makeshift shelter. I could almost picture his face, not sure whether to smile or be concerned. I heard him slip out of his shoes and take off his coat. I heard him kneel on the floor outside. He knocked on the hardwood, and I told him to come in.

Parting the blankets, your father stooped inside and took a seat on the pillow opposite me (I was expecting him!). He looked around at the fort's interior. He was impressed. "Festival of Booths?" he said, and I nodded, and he said, "Of course." I gotta say, kid, you taught us how to make one hell of a fort.

"I never understood," your father said, "why *booths*, why we were compelled to go forth and live in *booths*. What the hell did ancient Hebrews know about booths?"

"Joshua thought it might have been a mistranslation." Your father's perfume was filling the pillow fort with a sweet and manly smell. "Like how Elijah was said to have been fed by ravens, *orebim*, when really he was in all likelihood fed by *Arabim*, Arabs."

Your father made a staccato humming sound in his chest, and nodded.

"Less interesting that way," he said. "Better with the ravens."

"I agree!" Not perfume. Cologne. "That was Joshua's point. It's a better story if Elijah is fed by ravens, even if it makes no sense. It infuses wonder into the retelling. Makes Elijah and, consequently, *us* somehow more special. Even if it defies all logic. Because we don't tell stories for logic and reason. That's what life is for. We tell stories for the opposite of that."

It was about that time that the cat turned traitor and stretched her way across the fort to sit in your father's lap. We sat silently and watched until the cat had completed her maneuver.

"He was so good at breaking things down like that," I said. "Everything could be made into something simple. Do you remember, how when he didn't agree with something one of us said, he'd just raise his hands and show us his palms?"

"I do."

"He wouldn't speak against us, but he'd let it be known he was in protest."

"Naomi does the same thing. Only she just slams a door somewhere."

We both laughed. Then I showed him the newest letter from your sister. He read it for a while, going over it twice before setting it down on the cat.

"So I guess that's that," he said.

"Looks that way." Then I added, "I'm proud of her."

"I am, too."

"Yes. But still."

He reached over to touch my leg. But he had to scoot forward to do it, tipping toward me on his knees, and the cat tumbled with zero grace from his lap onto the floor. So much for our bittersweet moment of parenthood. It's hard to be stoic and sad in the company of a cat whose dignity's been stained. And anyway, laughter and crying so often look the same. Why not trade? I wiped my eyes while the cat flurried out from our blanket fortress, and when my hiccups finally stopped, I put it as plainly as I can.

"I miss our kids."

"Me too. They're sweet."

I might have still been hiccuping.

"One still is. Even if she is far away."

"They both are." He smiled up at the patchwork quilt spread above us as our roof. Like there was something there that I couldn't see. Constellations among the stitches. Then he smiled back at me. "What's sweeter than a child who never grows up?"

Kheshvan 15, 5757

THIS AFTERNOON, JUST NOW, THE CAT SAT UP WITH A START from her sleep in the bright sunny patch on the hallway floor. It was like she was watching some unseen thing zipping toward her from the living room. She raised her hackles and gave one warding meow (the first she's made in the house!) and bolted for the bedroom and under your father's bureau. So I guess all three of us believe in ghosts now.

Kislev 25, 5757

I CAN'T TELL IF YOUR FATHER IS ENDEAVORING VALIANTLY to make things up to me or if there's been a deep and fundamental change in him—my honest guess is that Naomi's now-permanent far faraway-ness is at least partway to blame, nailing home the point that the years could not, that it's *just the two of us now* (of course, then again, the change could in fact be completely within me, the governing body of my soul changing its policies without my even knowing it, irritability exchanged for humor, frustration swapped for patience, the sum total inviting your father closer to me instead of further away: who's to say!)—but whatever the reason, I'm taking it. He's helping with dinner and lighting candles on Fridays. He's taking me to movies. He's fun! It's been so long since his clowning's been for anyone's benefit but his own. I'd forgotten what a riot he could be (it's distracting—I get excited an hour or two before he's due home from work—so distracting I sometimes forget that I have a ghost son with whom to correspond). And I am one hundred percent willing to accept the possibility that maybe he's been performing his husbandly duties to the fullest all along and it's *me* who's been a brooding drip. But however you slice it, this sure does feel like a second courtship (and isn't that what life after kids is supposed to be? a second marriage without the mess of a divorce?). And the crowning stupidity of it is, this unexpected togetherness makes me miss him all the more. You'd think a feather blew through my car, the way I weep these days. What even do I think I'm missing? He's right here! Shooting me with rubber bands and begging me to sing "Lay Lady Lay," which is a confusing request but one oddly thrilling to grant. Eagerly game for whatever I might propose. Even remembering—I can hardly believe it—an honest-to-God holiday. Last night, at his urging, we gambled for M&Ms (apparently, he couldn't find chocolate gelt at the Wegmans). Anted up and spun the bone. Absolutely acting like a couple of little kids. Stealing candy and stealing turns. It was impossible to tell who was winning. Neither one of us could help eating the pot.

Tevet 22, 5757

YOUR FATHER SPENT THE MORNING FOLLOWING THE CAT FROM room to room. This made her more active than usual. She examined things she'd never before cared to sniff. She rubbed against doorframes and batted dust bunnies beneath the bed. She didn't want him to think she wasn't busy!

Shevat 1, 5757

LAST NIGHT BROUGHT A HARD STORM AND THIS MORNING, A LITTLE more snow succeeded to fall. To me, it was a beautiful thing to wake up to—the unmarred stretches of undulating blue stretching out to welcome the naked black trees, the dense wool of sky, the cinematic drift of the last few unhurried flakes—but your father was a little less in love with the scene that greeted him this morning. The plows had totally buried his car in a bank of hardened slush and crusty road salt and ice. He took one look through the frosted kitchen window, then bitterly wished for spring. My car, however, was fine. I drove your father down to the train station and saw him off (his company's been sending him more and more often up to Syracuse and Albany and Rochester for reasons I wonder if even your father understands), then very carefully drove home, the roads having been sanded more than plowed and so gripless most of the time and black-iced the rest, and it was along the way that I saw your idiot friend's parents. They were walking side by side—or anyway, they were trying to, but since the sidewalks hadn't been cleared, their options were to either tromp through the fresh snow or walk single-file in the narrow lane stamped down by the few walkers before them, though it appeared they were attempting to do both at once, each with one foot in the path and one foot slogging through the new crunchy fluff—and from the looks of things, they were heading home from an early trip to the grocery store: she was carrying a single plastic bag in one mittened hand while he held an over-sized can of what I took to be fruit cocktail, cradled in one arm between his chest and the crook of his elbow. It seemed a little too tender of a maneuver to be treating a can of fruit. Because the roads were bad, I passed them real slow, and it was likely for this reason alone that I even recognized them. I do not often see the Nigras around—they have always struck me as a quiet family, maybe not necessary secretive, but not necessarily *not* secretive either—and as far as I can recall, I only ever spoke to the mom once or twice, both times over the phone, that one fall their son insisted on hanging around. I do not think I've ever heard the father's voice, and I certainly don't know their names. But I recognized them. Her red-brown curls clouding out from under her homemade watchman's cap. His spiky crown of black cowlicks (no hat for him, I guess) waggling in the wind. Both of them grey-eyed, both pale, both tired-looking. Honestly, they looked more like siblings, or anyway, cousins, than like husband and wife. And even in memory, I can see the shape of their son's sallow face clearly reflected in their faces, though I doubt I could say what features he inherited from whom.

I watched them struggling in their snowy walk home, and I said the word aloud: "Delinquents."

I don't know why this struck me today as being important, seeing these two laboring in the snow with their meager supply of groceries. I've since come home and had a second cup of tea and fed the cat and listened to the news on the radio, yet behind all of this, like the pitted white wall against which a film is projected, I see these two people, heads down, marching home. I don't know why the sight of them is important to me right now. I've likely driven past the Nigras countless times—it's not that big of a town—stood in lines with them at the bank and post office, held open doors or had the door held open for me, and not once have either of them stuck in my memory. But today, easing slowly down the icy black scratch of Riser Avenue, tires throwing up that useless sand-slush-paste, *everything* is there for me. The weird orange and brown plaid of her mackinaw. His grey canvas jacket—really too light for this kind of weather—like something a mechanic would wear. The blue shadow of his stubble. The tired set of their mouths. Her free arm was stretched out to her side, nearly perpendicular to her body for balance. He, meanwhile, walked like a stray dog. If he had a tail, it'd be between his legs. And I remember, his head was inclined toward hers, like he was saying something quietly for only her to hear. But his lips didn't move. Only his breath puffed icily around his face. I remember seeing that giant can of fruit cocktail, held like a sleeping infant against his chest, and thinking of the viscous syrup inside, of the too-bright cherries and slick slices of peach, the pale and mealy slabs of pear, and feeling a little shiver of revulsion. I wondered why they were walking and not driving in the face of such bluster and bone-chill. I wondered if they still lived in their rundown house in the woods at the edge of town. I remember thinking: it's a long walk in the snow.

I have absolutely no reason to blame their son—and, by extension, *them*—for your death. I have zero reason to believe *anyone* responsible. But I guess a whole lot of my life is lived in the absence of sufficient evidence. To stick to demonstrable truths doesn't provide me with much more than a tight dark box to tick off my days within. And I don't think I'm quite ready for that particular coffin yet. Which doesn't leave me much else as an option: proof or no proof, I have to continue living. I have to believe all sorts of things for which I have no proof. And I know, it's very likely that you could have lived your whole life safely indoors, hermetically sealed and slathered in bug spray and never once venturing down to splash and run in the buggy mire alongside that creek behind your idiot friend's house, and you'd still one day have grown pale and cold and fallen deeply into a sleep, resting lightly in the sterile white of your bed in the ICU—the nurses scratching their impotent heads while your doctor failed to arrive—before thrashing though a storm of seizures, jaw clenched tight so your brand-new molars cracked and the IV ripped meanly from your arm, only to then grow calm and still again and stay still and then stay still some more. This is an alternative route that you could very well have followed, that we could have followed, a road leading to the exact same hospital end. That's possible. But I've no reason to buy into that fantasy, either.

It was early yet so the sky was a dark winter-morning blue—the streetlights still burning, their cast yellow pools encroached tightly in icy-blue snow—and as I passed the pair of delinquent parents, I flashed my eyes up toward the rearview mirror just long enough to see the father drop his can of cocktail. They both stopped and stared down at where it'd fallen. Neither made a move to pick it up. I don't know how, but somehow, I was certain: the can had split open on the ice.

Shevat 15, 5757

It's called the New Year for Trees, and I suppose in Babylon this made a lot of sense. But here there are cubits of snow and the streetlights never turn off even during the day. The roads are pressed black with ice and the snow banks are grey and filthy. The crows are too cold even to scream. Over the Lakes, it's said, another storm is brewing, while already the birch trees are bent in half and snapping everywhere beneath their loads of snow and ice. For them, the New Year is no year at all.

And I swear, sometimes, your father is so dumb it hurts. I've lit the candles and set the table with figs and apricots and olives and nuts and honey, and he comes home with a god-damned pizza. But at least when he sees me waiting at the table, he knows to put the pizza away in the oven. He corrects quick, and he's been so much better these past few months, but still. I wish he could remember.

I know it's not his fault. He doesn't practice (I have to remind him sometimes, he's a Jew too, goy last name aside). With no temple and no community here in town, I barely celebrate either. But these reminders, in my own home, sometimes make me feel so alone.

At any rate, he seemed pleased with the fruit and the olives and the almonds. He said this was the way to eat. I poured us tall glasses of red wine, and that seemed to please him, too. We ate and told jokes and the cat came to bat at our toes under the table. The wind rocked against the house and snow sizzled against the windows. But we were inside. Not every celebration needs to be raucous. It's okay to speak softly in our joy. When the food was gone and the bottle was empty, I stood and walked slowly around the table to your father. The cat followed. Beneath my dress, her tail wrapped around my calf. I bent and kissed your father on both of his ears, and he stood and kissed both of my ears, and what we did next is no one's business but our own.

Shevat 23, 5757

It's late and it's Friday but your father still isn't home. He's in Syracuse I guess or has maybe now finally caught a train bearing him briskly toward home. His meeting ran overlong so that he missed the train he'd meant to catch, and then he missed the next one, too—his fault this time—so our date night out ended up being just me all alone. Not that we had big plans bannered all across the sky or anything. But that doesn't really have much to do with disappointment, does it? I made a light supper (just a piece of broiled whitefish overtop a green salad), and after washing up and sitting for a minute staring sightlessly at a crossword, decided I'd go to the damn movie anyway, date or no date.

I don't know if you'd remember the old Chanticleer Theater downtown. That's where the community drama club would have staged its lame productions of *Romeo and Juliet* and *Our Town* back when you were around. In the late 80s, the theater changed hands, and all the rows of folding seats were ripped out and replaced with tables and chairs and cheap-looking tablecloths, and a truly awful dinner theater began. That only lasted a couple seasons. Then for five or six years, the space was vacant. But just recently a couple from the city moved here and reopened the theater as a sort of art house. Every couple weeks, there's something new showing, alternating between strange foreign films (usually very sexual) or old black and whites I've never heard of before. In a town as small as this, you'd think it'd make for an even worse business venture than the dinner theater, but it's proven to be a much-loved (possibly much-needed) addition to the community. Maybe people are just tired of fiery explosions and Adam Sandler yelling like a toddler. I know I find myself coming here more often than the first-run theater out by the outlet malls. Last week, your father and I watched a movie about an Irish girl caught up in a deplorable marriage with a paralyzed oil-rigger (the girl believed she could talk to God). Which meant this week would be an old American movie. Your father prefers these. It's a shame he missed his train.

I arrived at the Chanticleer early (the new owners restored the old name, another hot move as far as opening a business in any small town: keep the gilded-nostalgia angle sharp) and so sat by myself up in the balcony and drank a plastic cup of wine (the options at the concession are simply "red" and "white," which doesn't bode for high expectations but often prove surprisingly good) and it was likely because of this that I kept nodding off throughout the movie. The gist of the spare plot (this was filmed in New York in the 50s) is that one boy, maybe ten years old, with his buddies convince his little brother, who's maybe all of six, that he— the little brother—has shot and killed his older brother in a weedy dirt lot behind their tenement building. Freaked out and ashamed, the little brother runs away to Coney Island, where most of the resultant movie takes place. Eventually, the older brother makes an obligatory, half-assed attempt at finding his missing kid brother. Not so much out of worry or love. Mostly to avoid getting in trouble with their mom (their father, apparently, is long and mysteriously dead).

This, anyway, is what I think the movie was about. Like I said, I kept drifting off to sleep. Which isn't to say I was uninterested. I actually really loved the movie—this little boy, from the very first scene, radiated a particularly acute and rending hurt that only a child can feel and express, inarticulate and unfiltered and really just *raw*, so much so that

I wonder now if he, the child actor, was even acting, if he knew he was in a movie at all, if maybe instead the directors had convinced him that he really had killed his brother—so much did it feel like a documentary—and maybe it was because of this I kept falling asleep without realizing, shifting seamlessly between the movie and my dreaming of being in a theater, watching uncolored images of fratricide and trickery flickering across the screen.

I'm not sure I could even really repeat the story of the movie as it was meant to be told. Nor that I'd want to. But clearly I feel compelled to tell you something about it. I remember that it began with the older brother apologizing for some previous injury exacted in the prehistory of the film (the older brother running up from some alley to say that he didn't know it'd hurt, then the younger brother, kneeling on the pavement with a piece of chalk, drawing horses, correcting him: "It hurts every time"), then the older brother and his buddies being bullies—something to do with not giving the little brother a turn, but mostly what I remember is the feel of the streets, the weedy vacancy of an unused lot strewn with trash, balled-up newspapers and empty bottles of Coke, the cramped matrix of alleys hemmed in by brick walls, the sky always a dull gradient of flat pressed lead—then a shot of the older brother pouting in a kitchen chair, the little brother holding a comic book and standing too near, the older brother sneering and delivering a vicious shove. I remember comprehending this little boy wanting—needing—desperately just a scant quarter-ounce of love or kindness or affection and getting the exact opposite instead.

I remember the little boy holding a cap rifle—the sky beyond him that same leaden weight, far-off power lines and a single water tower on the horizon—while one of the bullies coaches him how to fire, laying it on thick: "This is a live round, Joey, you could really hurt someone, somebody could even die."

The rifle firing and the older brother falling down, a smear of ketchup across his chest.

The little brother's face—heavy brows, freckled up-turned nose—collapsing in recognition: he's killed his older brother.

I guess then I dreamed for a while of that lost city. The scent of trash and exhaust. Pop caps skittering toothily against concrete. Cats on fire escapes. The little brother running. The street-noise of car horns and shouts, the rumble of trains coursing beneath the pavement. I saw the pink wads of bubble gum crammed into the sidewalk cracks. I saw bricks and bricks and bricks. I saw the little boy looking dangerously small, sitting on a bench in an empty subway car. I saw him run out the folding doors. The lazy turn of a seagull beneath a colorless sky. The chuck of train-wheels versus the tracks. I saw a sign for Coney Island.

Since it's black and white, it was the movie again and not my memories of Coney Island from when I was a kid. Crowds of people but since there's a lot of adults, it's mostly just knees and butts, the occasional downward-leering face. Horrible animatronic clowns rocking and flailing—even as a kid, I never understood what these were about, what they were for, how anyone could interact—each galvanized in tinny canned laughter. The sideshow barkers never exactly friendly as they caught your eye and shouted their spiel, not really much at all like real people and more like the laughing machines, horrible goblins manifest in our world so far removed from the fairytales. This place is scary, but it is also magical, and though the boy is contrite for the murder of his brother, he is also a little boy on Coney Island. He forgets. He cannot help but forget. The little boy gets on a carousel and tries to grab the brass ring as he spins past, and this is the first time he really looks happy, smiling, his heavy fish-lipped frown finally, fleetingly, gone. He almost falls off his rising/falling horsy as he reaches, failing to grasp the ring. He's laughing, then—you can see it happen, the exact moment it happens—he remembers: he's killed his older brother. His head falls and he hugs the pole running through his horsy. His face twists with messy tears. He nearly falls again as he slides off the saddle, trying to get away.

Then this scene just repeats itself, again and again and again. The boy stands in an alley, throwing rocks at a can. He tries his hand at a batting cage. He watches through a chain-link fence as honest-to-God ponies trot and run. He beams with the simple joy he discovers without a single kindred soul in the world. Then: he remembers. It hurts every time.

In the end, of course, the older brother finds him, does his best (though not really his best) to make amends. He runs around a lot shouting his brother's name. Mostly, he just mopes about the trouble he'll get into when his mom finds out what he's done. It's completely accidental when the brothers finally reunite on a stretch of beach made vacant by a sudden rain, though really, it might as well be a repeat of the very first scene. The older brother, relieved though vastly unapologetic, runs up to his brother standing in the sand and tells him: "It was only a joke." Meaning: I didn't know it would hurt. And the little brother, fishy lips frowning, wide-set eyes scrunching deep into shadows, moans (his voice is unsettlingly so low), "Why didn't you tell me?" By which it's understood: it hurts every time.

I don't know if this is how the movie ends or not. It could have kept going. But I wouldn't know. I was gone. I fell again into the deep woolly warmth of sleep and I did not dream this time and when I woke up, the theater lights were up and everyone else was gone. Deep in my belly lay the hard cold ache that I only feel when I first wake up from a nap—ever since college, I've never found myself more depressed than in the first few moments after waking from a nap, an incomprehensible loneliness wrapped up in a sense of failure, of dread, none of it definite or tied to any one thing yet nevertheless feeling proven, feeling correct, every pathetic step of my life leading up to this very moment, dumb and drooly and waking up on the couch (again) or waking up on a bus or waking up in a theater (again, again, again), the feeling of defeat almost crippling, at least until a few minutes later when I finally, fully wake up—and more acutely than ever, feeling that ache high up in my balcony seat, I wished your father was here. I wanted his smell. I wanted his giant hand to hold onto. I wanted. But I wasn't going to get it. I got up and threw away my wine-streaked cup—the crushed red fake velvet on the walls and steps down from the balcony making my footfalls sound both muffled and loud—and then walked home with the sharp breath of January stinging in my eyes and my cheeks. I came inside and found your father still not home. The cat asleep in a tight warm cue on the couch. The silence in the house a presence unto itself. I sat at the table and stared at the clock. Then I started a letter to you. There are so many things you never got a chance to know. So I get to know them for you. It's important that I let you know, kiddo: it hurts every time.

Adar II 1, 5757

I KNOW WHY THE CAGED BIRD SINGS. BUT WHAT ARE ALL THESE starlings so upset about?

Adar II 14, 5757

I LIKE IT WHEN YOUR FATHER PLAYS ALONG. LAST NIGHT WE GOT dressed up in our finest evening wear so that we didn't even look like ourselves anymore. Then we went down to the pub on the corner, the one with the stupid Polish name. We were so out of place there! We ordered burgers and beers and deliberately got loopy and it wasn't even dark yet outside. I recited the story of Esther by memory (or anyway, told it like family history, some not-so-secret gossip about your great aunt so-and-so) and your father booed emphatically each time I said Haman's name. The crowd in the bar could not stop staring. We were actually asked to leave! Afterward, we walked to the wine store and ordered a bottle to be sent to your doctor's house, the way we do every year, as he is someone we must forgive and forgive again (we very likely should have sent something to the Nigras, as well). Then we headed home. But on the way we met a homeless man who asked us for some change, and instead, we bought him new clothes. Walked him straight into the only clothing store in town and had him try on new jeans and some shirts he could layer up. Then we took him to a pizza place and bought him a meatball sub. None of this seemed to faze him. Like it really wasn't all that uncommon for strangers to now and then take an interest in his plight. He was young and had lost a few teeth, which made him move his mouth in a funny way to hide the gaps. He did not eat like he was ravenous. He took his time to enjoy his root beer and sub. Then again, maybe he ate slowly because of his missing teeth. It should have felt weird, sitting across from this stranger, your father and I, all dressed up and saying nothing and watching him eat. But all of it made a sort of sense.

When he was done, he wiped his mouth carefully with a napkin and folded his sandwich paper into a tight square. Then he put the square and napkin inside his empty cup. None of us ever shared our names. All we knew about him was that his own father had conned him out of his meager life savings, then later stole his checkbook and wrote a lot of bad checks in his name, so he now has a criminal record that is not his own. It makes finding a job or a place to live nearly impossible. He has to make due with what few options he has left.

Your father said that he must hate his father for doing that to him. But the man just shrugged. "If it wasn't for him," he said, "I would've never met you nice people." Then he stood up and thanked us for dinner, and threw out his cup, and was gone.

Adar II 15, 5757

Found a thank you card waiting in the mailbox this afternoon. No postmark. Hand-delivered. Your doctor. Sharing his quiet gratitude for the wine. And I can't even say his name.

It's a sad state of affairs when you find yourself wishing you were more like a homeless man.

Adar II 16, 5757

Dear Ghostie,

I hate admitting this to you, kiddo, but I sometimes dream that you come back. I don't mean like we're all in the hospital gathered around your bed waiting for the inevitable when all at once your fever breaks and your pulse picks up, your skin lightly pinkens with the sunburn you lost and you at last open your bright and criminal eyes. No. You die. In my dreams, you die and have been dead for years. But then, without warning, you're back. There's never an explanation. You're dead and dead and suddenly at a train depot or at your sister's graduation or on the dusky summer streets outside the carnival, you're not. You're alive. You haven't aged and you haven't changed. *But we have!* And that's the worst part. Knowing just how much we have to explain.

In my dream last night, it was the rainy season. Your father and sister and I were living in a clapboard house in a small town out west somewhere. The street outside our windows was a river of bubbling red clay, moving fast and wrinkled with rain. It all seemed like a long time ago. We were engaged in our domesticity, brewing coffee, chasing the cat. It wasn't a very interesting dream. But then you showed up. Wiping the rain from your hair and smiling. You seemed happy to inexplicably be alive and as usual, we were all taken aback, everyone trying to act as normal and casual as you, never acknowledging the great quivering sense of wrong vibrating in our chests.

Your father and sister found some reason to go do something in the rain and left us at home together alone. Which should have been what I wanted. On a dusty green divan in our (I don't know what the room was, so I'll just call it a) parlor, you made yourself comfortable with your legs folded and crossed, and you started in on one of our favorite old arguments. And what's amazing is, after all these years, it was the same argument we always had back before you died. About the world that is and the world to come. You quoted Rabbi Yaakov's assertion that it is better to spend just one hour in this world repenting and doing good deeds than to spend all one's life in the world to come doing so. And it's better to have only one hour of tranquility in your whole entire life here in this world than to spend all your life in the world to come in peace and calm. The rabbi's point, you suggest, is almost Christian, that we must spend this life enacting *mitzvahs* in order to spend the next in blissful reward. Which sort of makes the *mitzvahs* insincere. But that, you said, is beyond the point. Because if we have only our deeds and experiences in this world to go on, then the world to come doesn't matter. We can't know what happens there. And it very well may never come anyway (after all, you said, it hasn't yet). Only this world matters. So, you concluded, it is better to spend your life in repentance and doing good deeds than in any sort of tranquility. The world to come doesn't need to exist for this life to be lived well. Which is just another way of saying that there is no world to come.

You sat there on the dusty green divan, looking up at me, eyes like flints of melting ice and your wet hair winding in ever-tightening curls, waiting for me to assert my usual claim to the contrary, that the world to come does need to exist, that this life means nothing if there isn't something better ahead. But I was too tired to play this game. I stared at you and hoped you'd see without my having to explain the irony of a little dead boy come back from the grave to tell me there is no world to come. When I realized you couldn't and wouldn't see on your own, I got up and left the room. I picked up the cat and stood by the kitchen window. The cat purred and nuzzled under my chin. I watched the falling rain flood our town.

You know that I love you, Joshua. You know I miss you. But sometimes, honestly, I wish you'd leave me alone.

In a while, I got you dressed in dry clothes and an oilskin coat and we walked through town until we came to a potter's field. Your father and sister were there and so was everyone else. There was a big commotion out there in the rain. Men with shovels were slogging deeper down into the red muck of our town. There'd been a mistake. Two men had been accused of some crime, had been sentenced to be buried alive. But new evidence has since come to light. The men must be dug up and set free. Even if what we set free is dead. Lay us down to sleep, Adonai. In peace, raise us erect to life. Spread over us the shelter of your peace. The accusers will be buried instead.

Constellations on a String
2001

There is glass between Ben and the world. It is a fever of retreating shadows, fading faces and reaching hands, and there is glass between Ben and the world. The reaching hands never touch him. The faces cannot clearly be seen. A dark-haired girl reaches her hands toward him and his parents each reach their hands toward him and in a vague shadow play, the shapes of two boys stand up from their desks and walk out through a door, stand up and walk out, leave and leave again. There's the stain of dust and the shape of graves and when Ben reaches his own hands to touch the dividing glass, the fugue shatters and he's awake.

But really, it's the hiss of released brakes that wakes him. On a city bus shelter's bench, Ben opens his eyes and leans forward, peers past the shelter's graffitied plexiglass, but there is nothing to see. The faint red of a traffic light in the fog to his left. The faint green of a traffic light in the fog to his right. Dark grey street within the greater swallow of grey. As if this infant world is still being born. Leaning back into the bench, Ben closes his eyes, slips easily back into an animal half-sleep. He doesn't know or care how long he's been waiting on this bench. He's in no rush to get where he's going.

It is a vague and early morning hour. Ben is dressed in a navy blue jacket and slacks, a white shirt and no tie. At his feet rests a slim brief case and across his chest, a bulky leather satchel is slung. In the briefcase are papers and notebooks, pencils imprinted with the shapes of his teeth. The satchel contains a Marantz tape recorder and microphone and a dozen archival audiocassettes. His clothes have a worn looseness like maybe they're second-hand or like maybe he's lost weight. He has not changed his clothes in days. He wiles and catnaps through this misty dawn as he has countless dawns before because he is terrified of going home. If asked, he knows he wouldn't be able to explain why. Not because he doesn't know. Because he doesn't want to admit that he does.

In the fog, the lights change color. Then they change again. An old woman dressed in faded shades of blue slowly manifests from the morning's grey, down the sidewalk and to the space beside Ben on the bus shelter's bench. It's possible she's the one—or anyway, one of the ones—who's been watching him. Taking account of his movements. Waiting. But he doubts it. Ben wakes enough to smile a greeting to her, but a self-consciousness keeps him from falling back to sleep—it seems like a rude thing to do, and anyway, her being there ruins what calm he's found in solitude: being near a person has ruined his calm—so he sits up and stays awake.

An unseen door opens and closes. In the fog, a single bird whistles a tune, then stops. There's a pregnancy in the air before the old woman speaks. Ben knows it will happen before it does.

"You're that man, aren't you?"

Her voice is like a played out zipper, too slowly unzipped. It's the sound of decades and the sound of need. The anxious knot of Ben's organs twists a little tighter, but he smiles and nods and by the way she smiles back, he knows: she's convinced.

"I've seen you around," she says. "With your microphone? You recorded my friend Mel's stories last month. Mel Goldfarb?"

"Yes," and he nods. "I remember Mel. He's a charming man."

"He told you about his wife and kids, right? That's what he told me when I asked about you. I saw you leaving his building one time. We live across the street from each other, Mel and I. We sometimes see each other at the same deli during lunchtime. He said that you wanted to know about the summer vacations he and his family would take out at Skaneateles."

"That's right," Ben says. "Mel had many good times with his family out there, and I wanted to know all about it." But Mel never once mentioned Skaneateles to Ben, never mentioned his family at all. Sitting across from one another at a narrow table in the old man's yellowed efficiency—the microphone poised like an insect between them—Mel told Ben of his time in the service during the Second World War, when he worked as a guard at an internment camp in northern California. Of the relationships he'd built there, with the other guards and with the inmates. Of the things that happened within the walls strung high with angled lines of barbed wire. He hadn't been troubled by the work at the time. He'd felt like a patriot, like he was protecting his country from a conspiracy of spies and traitors. He maintained that belief for years after the war. First because he did believe it. Then later because he could not admit otherwise. But the years revealed his truth as a lie that he continued to believe until he could not deceive himself anymore. "For a long time after that, I just stopped talking about it." Ben remembers, a steady tremor moved through Mel by the time he finished telling his story. "Much later, I'd tell people that I'd been a conscientious objector. That I'd worked at a labor camp until the war was over. Picking beans in northern California. That's what I still tell people now. It's easier to lie than admit what I done." Stacked on the floor beside Mel's chair rose a sloppy tower of newspapers. At his elbow, cutout cryptoquizzes scattered across the table. "Everyone who might know the truth is long dead. You're probably the only person alive who knows what really happened."

But Ben does not tell the woman any of these things. "Those were happy times for Mel," he says.

"Yes, they were." The woman digs inside her white woven handbag, gives up without finding anything. It's a nervous gesture, Ben knows. She isn't looking for a thing.

"Would you—?" she asks at last, and then blushes. "I mean, could I—?"

"Would you like to tell a story for me?"

And somehow, she blushes more. "Do you have your recorder?"

He taps the satchel laid across his lap. He smiles and unbuckles its flap. He does not need to withdraw the machine to connect the mic cable and insert a fresh tape. He starts the reel rolling and states the date into the microphone.

Ben turns the mic toward the old woman and smiles. He looks into her eyes. Sees what she was like as a little girl. As a young woman. As a mom and as a widow. Once you learn how to look at people, all these things are revealed. Every nerve and every muscle inside Ben's body is an electric and strung-tight line, sizzling and ready to snap, but his smile is a disguise that puts the woman at ease. She doesn't know who he is. She only knows what he shows her. She smiles back and trusts the man she sees.

"Will you say your name into the record?" he asks, and when she tells him—"Evelyn Walsh"—he says her name back to her—"Evelyn Walsh, Evelyn Walsh"—then invites her to begin: "Evelyn, I'm curious what you think about second chances."

THERE ARE RITUALS THAT PUNCTUATE BEN'S DAYS AND HIS LIFE. Building barriers around his uncertainties. Keeping the unknowns contained. Ben records Evelyn's story, then rides the bus through the mist-heavy morning. Gets off at the campus stop. Stands in the silence between empty buildings—no birds yet or cars, no wind to swish the leaves—then follows the familiar flagstone path through the growing light to the faculty gym. At the front desk, Ben signs in under the tired gaze of a work-study undergrad, then steps in among the warm chlorine steam and dripping tiles of the vaulting natatorium. The scent and heat and the lipping sound of water together make his already-exhausted mind feel that much closer to sleep, to dreaming. It's a comfortable feeling of floating before he's even in the water. He gazes for a moment into the lap pool's still, reflecting screen, then strips off his clothes in the locker room and descends naked into the warm and shallow therapy pool. This early, there is no lifeguard. There is no one here at all. None of these things are coincidence. On his back, Ben floats once slowly across the pool's length. Turns to make a second pass. Only gets halfway.

He bobs in the softly shifting water.

He lets out his breath, and he sinks.

So calm above, how is it so much calmer below? Ben comes to rest on the pool's blue floor, knees to his chest and arms around his knees, staring through the blue expanse as the water roars against his ears. It does not matter that he's only five feet under. He is at the bottom of the world. And the allure of staying is incredible. To remain forever in this warm and quiet embrace. To stare through the blue into the heart of the black well. To allow this silence to become him.

If there are goblins in the forest, then the ghosts live under the water. He sees their shadows passing through the paling blue light. They are slow and have their own agendas. But they do not see him here.

It feels like lifetimes pass before Ben rises and breaks the surface. But it's not a feeling that lasts. Lungs burning amazingly with their first sucking breaths: he's still alive. What more could he ever expect to be? Ben pulls himself from the pool and showers and dresses and once again must come to terms with having always to be the one who's alive.

AT HIS POST, THE UNDERGRAD SNOOZES WITH HIS FACE PILLOWED in his open history book—completely lost, he doesn't know that he isn't still reading—so Ben leans against the wall, slides to the floor, and for a while, like dogs in a pack, he and the undergrad sleep. The rising sun pushes back the fog enveloping the city. Weary gangs of students wander out to early classes or to the dining hall in dull-eyed stupefaction, hurrying home in yesterday's clothes from someone else's room. Occasionally, a professor passes unseen. Because the campus shares no visible liminal edge with the surrounding city, there are also people who are late to work, driving or walking or running for a bus. There are shops whose doors are about to open or are opening now. Convenience stores brewing cheap coffee. Diners frying eggs. All of this occurs over the course of a few minutes—while the undergrad dreams of Genghis Khan crashing a lakeside swimming party, while Ben dreams of a preying mantis tapping at its prison glass—the longest stretch Ben has slept in weeks.

They sheepishly awaken to the throat-clearing sound of a pair of tenured English professors standing over them, owl-brows in deep discussion, each man wanting seriously to swim. The undergrad signs them in. Ben slinks off to his class.

THIS WALKING BUSINESS WAS EASIER, BEN THINKS, BEFORE anyone else was here. It's not an issue of traffic. The world is just more comfortable to pass through when it's emptied of everyone else. Ben wonders if *quiet* he's always equated with *safe*.

But still, there are advantages to the sudden crush of people. Along the way to class, Ben bums a quarter and a dime from one of his students. Finds a payphone. Calls his landlady. She tells him that she never sees him around the building anymore. Tells him she's begun to worry. He never answers when she knocks. No matter how early or late she drops by. Never around. She insists: everyone is very concerned. She does not expound on the definition of "everyone." She reminds him that rent is due.

"I know, I'm sorry." The phone stands alongside a path cutting through the quad. In the newly exposed sun, every-one is squinting. Ben squints at the students squinting past. Above him, on the post that holds the phone, is a sign that reads PHONE. He reads the sign a few times before continu-ing. "Finals are coming up. It's a very weird time around here."

"Uh-huh. Sure. It's the *time* that's weird."

He asks about his mail. She says that there's definitely mail. "The slot's jammed with the stuff. It's piling up like some kind of volcano over here."

At the center of the quad, Ben sees the three flag-poles—the nation's and state's and university's banners snapping high in the wind—each wrapped in crepe rib-bons of blue and pink and white, fluttering and languid and somehow unreal.

"Has anyone—" and he pauses. Steadies his breath. "Has anyone stopped by? Anyone looking for me?"

But she doesn't get what he's asking. "Who'd be coming around, Ben? You don't even come around. Why would your friends come around when you ain't never home?"

Ben squints against the light. He squeezes the receiver in his hand. Grinds his teeth. The crepe ribbons rise and furl. He says he'll be by today to pick up his mail. That he'll drop off the rent soon. That she really shouldn't worry. He hangs up before she can say much more.

ON HIS WAY FROM THE PAYPHONE TO CLASS, BEN SEES A young woman loping through the shaded quadrangle grass. Slim and well-built, ponytail swishing along her long jogger's spine, all dark hair and dark eyes. Ben stops and watches her pass, books held close to her chest, until he cannot see her anymore. He stands looking after her long after she's gone.

Finally, more slowly than before, he continues across campus, downhill to the social sciences building set like a bunker deep into the steep edge of the slope. He enters at the top floor and descends to the lowest level of doctoral offices. Asks the division secretary if his advisor has come in today. Is not surprised to learn that he has not, that no one expects Dr. Rubens back at all, let alone this semester. Ben asks for the address of the rehab clinic. As he does every week. Writes it down and vows that he will not lose or intentionally misplace the address again. As he does every week. The division secretary smiles wanly as she repeats the street and room numbers. Ben thanks her and returns to the top floor.

So deeply embedded into the hillside, the whole building feels like a basement. Only the northern face looks out onto the steel-and-glass shoulders of the city. Ben stands before the tall sheets of window, gazing at the smog-stained brick, the smokestacks and radio towers, the cranes slowly deconstructing the rail-bridges no longer fit for use, waiting, watching time seep from every unlaid brick and unmoored girder until quarter past nine, when he turns to greet the few kids who've met him here in the lobby.

They've long outlived the need for a classroom. In just a few minutes, he'll have told them everything he has worth telling and they'll return to their actual lives. Coffee and friends. Cigarettes and secret anxiety. The busy work of unquiet minds. As he hands back the previous week's assignment—a five-page digest of what will ultimately be their final report—Ben encourages them to quit reading until the semester's out.

"You all have voices of your own. And you're all subjugating those voices for those whose work you admire. Agee or LeBlanc or, Jesus, even Matthiessen." Laughter scatters among the students. "Stop speaking through someone else's voice."

One student—a flattop junior who could actually graduate this year if he chose, pompous but intelligent—speaks up, challenges Ben to verify the theory that, by speaking in the authoritative voice of antiquity, one's piece can take on a canonical air, can be taken more seriously.

"Look. What is this class? We're studying personal anthropology. You're uncovering the history of yourselves. Interviewing family. Digging up your grandparents' immigration papers. You are each on an empirical exploration of your selfhood's prehistory. And you're asking for my permission to deny you your own voice while documenting this? No. You do not get my permission, Bret."

More laughter, more relaxed this time. The junior's face reddens, but he's smiling.

"Think of it this way. I know this man. A mechanic who runs a successful shop. His wife wants to become part of the modern culture. Free music and daily cat pictures. So she asks him to buy her a computer. Subscribe to high-speed internet. Et cetera. He can afford this, and he likes his wife, so sure. He grants her this request. Now, he's more the sort of guy whose spare time is spent tinkering on projects in his shop or in the yard. He's not the sort to stare at a screen, to hit buttons, but eventually he tries out his wife's new computer. And, as anyone will, he discovers internet porn." Among the boy students, a tense laughter quakes. "So now he's hooked. It's not just a masturbatory addiction. In his own mind, he's become a connoisseur. A student of every fetish and vice. It swallows all his time. The last time we spoke, he was raving about the emotional drama of this one particular site. Indebted husbands getting paid to watch their wives joyously lock hips with professional pornographers. This is what's replaced his mind and focus. Husbands weeping while their wives get their brains screwed out by gigantic strange men."

An uneasy ripple passes through the lobby. Ben wonders if he's lost them.

"The things you obsess on replace the things that you are. Stop reading Agee. Stop reading LeBlanc. Allow your own voice to emerge. Papers are due in one week. That means the 8th. No later than that. I'll be available for conferences in Dr. Rubens' office until maybe two o'clock today. I hope to see more than a few of you."

Released, they trickle out into the brightening day, and glancing once more out the towering glass screens—silent stacks and slowly unbuilding cranes—Ben heads to Dr. Rubens' office downstairs. Settles in among his absent mentor's spilling piles of books. The card catalog overwhelmed with ink-scrawled index cards. The hand-carved Balinese masks mounted high along the far wall. Sits and rests his hands on the desk's worn and pen-scratched face.

What he's doing—using a tenured professor's office as his own—is an obvious trespass. He knows this. Everyone knows this. But under these circumstances, who will stop him? The other professors turn a blind eye. The division secretary waves him through. Sitting at his mentor's desk, Ben fishes a notebook from his briefcase and sets it before him. Places the worn nub of a pencil in his mouth: wood and flaking paint. Closes his eyes and waits.

Ben sees a boy dismantling a radio.

A dark-haired girl swiftly crossing through the shade beneath tall trees.

Seed grass swishing against an open blue sky.

Figures in stairwells and figures in hospital halls.

Everything falling.

Slipping the pencil from his mouth, Ben opens his eyes and writes:

Joshua is the one that discovered the goblins. In the woods behind my house. He found their prints in the muck by the creek, sunken in where the last rain flooded the banks. He found the prints of their curved, mangled feet, but I didn't believe what he'd found. He lost his boot in the muck trying to prove it to me, but I didn't want to believe. So I ran home and left him there, fishing his boot from the creek by himself while the sun set all around him. I ran home and left him and when he finally appeared again in my backyard a half-hour later, he was shaken and moon-eyed and didn't say a word and I gave in and believed him. I used the outside spigot to hose the muck from his boot, then walked him home on the street-lit streets, and I believed. Whether I wanted to or not, I knew what was out there and knew it was real. But I never said I was sorry for running away. And now I wonder if I still believe. If I ever stopped believing.

If the horrors of the old world disappear to be replaced by the horrors of this new world, is it wrong for our faith to fade too? Would the old gods return if faith returned first?

Either way, Joshua, I'm sorry.

This is not part of Ben's work. This is the work behind the work. The framework underpinning the body of his graduate thesis. The thesis that, as things stand, no one will ever read. That he will never have a chance to defend. Yet even still, in his absent mentor's office—surrounded by the relics of his absent mentor's life—Ben continues with what he's begun. Sets another bone in the progressing skeleton of his memory. To wrap it in flesh and sinew. To create something more from what he's already lost. Even if this too must be lost.

BY QUARTER-TO-ONE, BEN GIVES UP. NO ONE IS COMING. No one has come. He has transcribed some of the new tapes, has begun integrating the new information into the existing text, but still: no one. Gathering together his things, Ben locks Dr. Rubens' office, nods polite good-bye to the division secretary at her desk, climbs the stairs to the top floor—tile and glass, smokestacks and falling bridges—steps out into the afternoon sun, and is blind. The sun is boiling bright and outpouring. The sky is a refracting lens. Ben stands blinking in the May Day sunlight, but he could just as easily be lost in the Sams' hallway floor's afternoon sheen. The whole world washed in white.

Suddenly eager to leave this place—its ancient brick and bowing trees, its young faces set with certainty and knowledge—Ben hurries off campus, impatient for the welcome anonymity of the city at large, the quiet of unpeopled streets, and it's when he's nearly free to roam among the pawn shops and vacant fronts and steaming manhole vents that someone calls his name.

"Mr. Nigra!"

A beacon or a bullet.

"Mr. Nigra. Hold up."

Flattop. Textbooks tucked against one breast. Free arm waving as he chases him down.

"Bret, sorry, hi."

"I was on my way to see you at your office."

"Not my office." The boy is young and cheery and an anchor dragging Ben down. "Conference hours are done for the day."

"I don't want to take up too much of your time."

"There's a pretty simple solution to that."

But even as he says it, Ben gives in. All red cheeks and a hopeful smile: how can anyone escape this?

"I just wanted to know how your story ends."

"You and me both. What story?"

"Your porno-friend. Whatever happened to him?"

As a boy, Ben would watch the playground games, knew how to play without ever having played. As a teen, he studied his peers' silent language of touch. Handshakes and subtle brushes. He was never invited in. Who would ever mistake him for anyone's friend?

"Nothing happened. He stopped helping around the house. He watched porn like a second job. The end."

"So it's happily ever after?"

"Right."

"Nothing else ever happened to the guy?"

Of all the students in his class—the curious anthropology majors ready to discredit any theory, the journalism students with sights set on *National Geographic*, clueless electives, the displaced and disoriented—this is, regrettably, Ben's favorite student. He's doing the work and doing it well. He regularly drops by for conferences. He challenges and likes to be challenged. He fills Ben with a bile that will not subside.

"Why do you care about this, Bret?"

"It's not a complete story. It's a partial history. A man gives up everything to dedicate himself to one ridiculous study. I want to know what happens when someone makes that sort of choice."

Ben scans the street. A rogue cab or bus. Any sort of savior.

"I'm not sure this is the sort of thing we should be discussing, Bret. I probably shouldn't have even brought it up in class."

Flattop laughs. Like he's heard this joke before.

"Didn't you say something at the beginning of the semester about all stories being valid? That all inquiries are simply a means of granting permission, allowing people to talk about their hidden histories?"

"How hidden is my history of being full of shit, Bret?"

But by the steady look the boy levels in response, Ben knows, there is no out.

The man's scholarship into digital fetish went on unabated for two years. At first his wife took it as a threat, then as an annoyance, then finally as a constant. He would need to be reminded more often of things she'd already told him. He might occasionally embarrass her in front of company with references to analingus and DPs. Even these things, too, she grew accustomed to, adjusting as any successful partnership must.

Like the gradual normalization of any steady change, this becomes the daily topography of their marriage. Then suddenly: an anniversary. Fifteen years. They survived the roulette of willful monogamy and consequent gambles: buying a home, raising children. What better way to commemorate than to go to Las Vegas? A less vice-heavy destination might have once made better sense, back in the days before the exploitation of flesh shaped the undercurrent running through their marriage. But maybe not. It could be that Las Vegas was the only place where they were ever designed to arrive. They fly to Nevada and descend into the scorched heart of the desert. Check into the air-conditioned subtundra of an infinitely stretching hotel. Lose themselves in the lights. Lose themselves in the simulated glamour. Lose themselves at a blackjack table and lose ten thousand dollars.

Which is to say, he loses ten thousand dollars. Though the money is both his and hers, part of their partnership, part of their success, he is the one that loses it. It's a slowly burning fuse, the rage that ignites in her. They cannot stay in their hotel. They cannot continue this journey. They check out with their bags and walk out to their rented car, and it's there in the parking lot that her fury detonates. Under the stars that cannot be seen for the superceding neon stars. Along tarmac still spongy from the day's heat. She loses it. Drops her bags. Screams her wrath upon him. It's not so much that he's lost the money as he's demonstrated quantitatively the depths to which he's a fuck-up. Every failure and disappointment—the life they vowed to build together versus the secure doldrums that account each day instead, the predictable house in the predictable suburbs, the predictable days, the predictable inability to change—finally has a venue for expression. This wasn't the life she was promised. She screams this in his face. Which attracts the attention of three men. Thick necks and expensive shirts. They're all of a mind, but only one speaks. Low in an untraceable accent. Makes an offer involving cameras and a free meal and a thousand dollars in cash. These men know who these unfortunate people are, and these unfortunate people know all about these men. The husband refuses but the wife accepts. This is how she punishes him. She will earn back a fraction of the money he has lost. The remaining balance, he will pay forever.

Of course, he can't leave his wife with these men. So he goes along with them. Which earns them another five hundred. He earns another five hundred dollars by watching while these strangers perform their venereal game with his wife. Becomes a character in this film by watching. Destroys himself by watching. His wife takes from it what she can.

"Jesus."

From behind Flattop, a city bus slowly approaches.

"Did they get a divorce after that?"

"What do you think?"

When the bus pulls up beside them, Ben hops on without saying goodbye to his student. Swipes his pass. Finds a seat near the back. For one fleeting second, he wants to shout something out the window about consequences, how every road taken bears its own toll. But more than anything, he wants this moment to be done. The brakes hiss and the bus glides into traffic. The road you don't take has its toll as well. The flattop junior disappearing behind him, Ben does not know where this bus will take him. He doesn't care where he'll end up.

THE SUN THROUGH THE WINDOW IS A HYPNOTIST'S FLAME. BEN sits and waits and with nothing to do, he closes his eyes. Like an animal dozing in the foyer, waiting for its master's return. Feels his mind grow hazy. Feels his heart speed up then slow. Breath low like something tidal. Aware of the people around him while aware too of the flicker behind his eyes.

The fade and bloom of faces, of figures.

A railroad carving through a forest, then a field.

A darkened room and a turntable.

A folded green shape at the bottom of a jar.

A long-gone afternoon lake-swimming with his parents.

He swam one way while they swam another.

He watched their splashing and knew their concern was only for each other.

He did not fit into their world.

The lens flare of memory starbursts off the water.

Falling leaves and falling water and falling hands.

Ben waits to arrive anywhere.

He practices the balance between.

THE BUS'S ROUTE ARCS GRADUALLY TO THE BROAD, EMPTY streets of the south end of town. Worn and dated neighborhoods sequentially claimed and abandoned by each successive immigrant class, Irish and Italian to Latino and

Somali. Ben steps out at a stop across the street from a halal market and a shop selling funeral suits—stiff jackets and paper shoes—and surveys the whole block for a pay phone, eventually scraping up enough change to call a person he knows hangs out around here. The voice that answers says he's at a basement fern bar on Hudson, between Sterling and Ontario, and Ben walks the few blocks alongside the canal chugging brackishly eastward, past kids swearing joyfully and a haggard man nursing a coffee on the levee. Ben knows: there's a lake out this way, and a small forest, too, hemmed in on all sides by houses and shops and vacant dusty lots. Cyclone fences. The occasional highway cloverleaf. Ben slips down the stairs into the bar between Sterling and Ontario.

Below street level, it's dark inside. All the ferns are dead. Crisp fronds drooping from long forgotten pots as something fiercely psychedelic by Jimi Hendrix howls through the sound system. There's a TV with a glowing blank screen high up in the corner and a tall man with only one hand standing behind the bar, but it's the man sitting at the counter that Ben is here to see. Hawaiian shirt and vague stubble. Everything pale and out of focus. A beer glass and a cell phone and an ashtray on the bar. The man looks up as Ben approaches, and his grin is not friendly and is also not a grin.

"Why hello, Mr. Ben." Voice leaping wildly between gravel and scraping slate. A free-baser's rasp. "Fancy seeing your face here."

Ben settles onto the neighboring stool and tries to get the bartender's attention—they're the only two patrons in this dim beery hole—but the bartender will not see him, in fact stands as far from them as he can without leaving altogether. The Hawaiian shirt man laughs and reaches behind the bar, pours a lager from the tap and sets it before Ben.

"Lefty here's become a little standoffish ever since I claimed this post as my new office. Hain't ya, Lefty?"

The bartender doesn't respond. Neither does Ben. The man swirls the foam of his beer with a swift twitch of his wrist, drinks deeply, finally asks Ben what he's doing here.

"I really just had a few questions."

"Ah, questions." The man fishes a cigarette from his breast pocket. "More questions." He draws out the vowels like he's enjoying the taste. "A man with questions arrives but says nothing." Strikes a blue-tipped match splitting into flame. "Waits to be asked about his questions." Exhales long and blue. "Just keep your tape deck where it is, alright, Genius?"

His aren't those sorts of questions, not this time, but he doesn't argue. Ben watches the smoke slowly sink to form a dense atmosphere just above eye level, dividing the room in half—the world above, the world below—while the man starts in telling a story about being invited up to a friend's apartment to see a kid get beaten. "I didn't know that that's what I was being invited up for, right? It was like a surprise. For me!" The kid was duct-taped to a chair in the kitchen. Mouth sealed shut and fear beaming from his eyes like sudden headlamps in the night. A bunch of folks were gathered around to watch and this one guy who looked like the famous actor from all those movies that were really plays kept pacing the room like a jungle cat in a cage, but the lighting was all wrong. Not a lone naked bulb swinging from a ceiling wire but good warm buttery kitchen light. "The vibe was less like a beating and more like a holiday party. Like, this was Christmas dinner. What's this asshole doing all tied up?" Everyone was relaxed and easy. Except for the guy in the chair. Except for the pacing man, who must have known that he looked like the famous actor because when he finally spoke, it was in monologue, a surprisingly eloquent speech about the fate rats bring down upon themselves when they choose to narc out friends, choose to help the police arrest friends. "I remember, he kept talking about loyalty, like the real offense here was the guy letting down his pals, you know, breaking their trust. Like the arrests were secondary to him being a shitty friend." The man in the chair squirmed. Someone passed around some popcorn. "Everything felt so cozy, you know. It was a real jolt when the kid's jaw got broke." The man who wasn't the famous actor had been occasionally, like punctuation, strik-ing the boy throughout the speech. When he reached his climax—"'Why would you make us feel this way?' he kept shouting, 'Why would you make us want to feel this?'"— he grabbed a rolling pin from the counter and struck the boy twice in the head. Both times, something crunched and squirted blood out the kid's nose and ear. The second blow toppled the chair. The man who wasn't the actor dropped the pin and grabbed hold of the chair, lifted it and the boy together in the air and slammed them to the floor. The chair shattered. The boy crumpled, belly-down and worming on the linoleum. The man who wasn't the famous actor knelt on the boy's back and punched him hard in the neck three times, then sharply bent both elbows the wrong way. First one. Then the other. "The way that kid's joints came undone," he says, stabbing out his cigarette on the counter beside the ashtray, "It sounds exactly the way you'd imagine it."

Apparently finished with his story, the man yells to the bartender to put the TV on his channel, and like he's suddenly switched on, the bartender complies, reaching up to adjust the knob with his one hand. On the once-blank screen, men on bicycles appear, laboring to ascend a mountainside. The man beside Ben rises in his seat, balancing on the crossbars of his stool, fists pumping. "Yeah! Fuck yes!" Beyond the bicyclists, Ben can see an old stone church, then a little graveyard, then some feathery trees. When the riders crest the hill, they fold in close to their bikes and sail down the other side. But the man beside Ben isn't interested in all that. After a minute, he tells the bartender to turn it off. Jimi's guitar continues to wail like a widow from a battlement wall. The man lights another smoke.

Staring at the man, Ben can see him as a boy, a mouthy little scrapper tough enough to back up his every threatening word. He probably had a cat he loved dearly that none of his friends knew anything about. Chances are good: he still does. While the man drags hard on his cigarette, Ben moves his mouth around the words, then finally says, "Thank you, Richard. But that wasn't what I was curious about this time."

The man blows smoke dismissively, wincing, waves his hand through the plume. "Hey, who gives a fuck, right? What's on your mind?"

Once while walking through the woods behind his parent's house, Ben stepped out into a field where swallows and dragonflies swarmed to feed on the afternoon's banquet of insects. Their motions so fluid and graceful and fine. Like machines built for this one purpose alone. This was the August after his freshmen year. Naomi was already gone. It felt no better the second time around. Often it was a numbness that subtly shaped his face and his mouth, his words and passage through space. Sometimes the weight of it was a crushing threat, though rarer still the weight became so much that somehow, it'd all reverse. His loneliness would become a balloon, lighter than air yet also filled with air. His loneliness would become a parachute. Ben stood at the edge of the grassy expanse and watched the swallows and dragonflies feed—elegant systems, circles and spirals—then walked out to stand among them in the middle of the field.

The worst they could do, he thought, was leave. Fly off to some other bug-ripe meadow. There was no way he could possibly be any more alone. But the birds continued to feed around him, sometimes so close, he swore they might hit him. The dragonflies continued to feed. And slowly it dawned on him that he meant nothing to these creatures. It didn't matter if he stood among them or not. No threat or comfort could he offer them. He was an absence around which they flew. Dead air. A vacuum. Among them, he became invisible.

But this is not what Ben tells the man. What he says is what feels like the truth, be it factual or otherwise. "I feel as though I'm being followed." He sees his shadow dragging from his feet, casting across a bootprint in the muck. He sees hunched silhouettes lurching among bare trees.

"Like every move I make is being tallied in some watchful accountant's ledger. That sounds more poetic than I mean it to. Someone is *watching* me. You know? I can *hear* the footsteps sometimes. Like they're just behind me and getting closer." It's saying the words aloud that reveals how true they might be. He looks at the man and sees goblins in the woods, and like something bad steaming in his belly, Ben feels his suspicions are true. "Have you mentioned me to anyone?"

The question within the question is obvious.

"Look." The man holds up his beer, gestures with it as he speaks. "I run a lot of deals, guy. Not all of them are good ones. You know? Maybe there are consequences I hope to avoid. Maybe I write my own insurance policy. Is it possible that sometimes, I use your name in place of my own?" He answers his own question by draining his glass and dropping it off the backside of the bar. Tiny glass eyes spray across the floor, peering wetly from the stained black wood. The one-handed man flinches. The man in the Hawaiian shirt stands and coughs and leaves without paying. This line of inquiry, clearly, is over. Laying down a few crumpled dollars, Ben follows him out onto the street.

"What happened to the kid after you guys beat him up?"

You guys. Because no observer remains passive for long. We all become culpable in time. The wind from a passing truck stirs the man's fading hair, ripples his played-out shirt. Squinting in the sun's stark light, he looks worn.

"I think we drew on him in black magic markers and

tossed him into a trash compactor behind an organic grocery store."

Briefly, Ben wonders what sort of life one must lead to find himself finally at the bottom of a reeking dumpster. But it doesn't take much wondering.

"If you saw him again—if that sort of thing were possible—is there anything you'd want to say to him? Anything you'd want to ask?"

The man makes a sort of laughing sound with his nose. "But that's the funny thing, now ain't it? I *do* sometimes see that little shit around." He smiles and for the first time, Ben can see: his teeth are edged in black. "Some fucks just don't know when to stay dead, you know?"

It could be argued, Ben thinks, that some people don't know when to stay alive either. But he knows enough to keep his mouth shut. If there's a softness in this man, right now, it's overwhelmed by something else. In statistics, it's called an outlier. The data point you disregard. Ben leaves the man standing on the sidewalk between Sterling and Ontario. It's likely less a question of *when* than *how*. How to stay dead. How to stay alive. When Ben looks back, the man's exactly where he left him.

Something else Ben's recorded in his journal, a memory dislocated from any timeline, something crucial but quietly so: he and Joshua galloping on all fours up and down the stairs of his house (this pointless game, he remembers, they called Dos Amigos Burritos). They thumped and galumphed in their ungainly race, and he remembers his mom telling them to be careful on the stairs, then reminding them again more sharply, then finally yelling at them, *be careful on those stairs*. As if that flight of thirteen steps was the most dangerous place in the house. And maybe it was. It's the only time Ben can recall his mother ever raising her voice in anger at him. But even then, he could tell, her anger was a mask for fear.

A CITY BUS STOPS BUT ROARS OFF AGAIN, NO ONE HAVING GOT on or off, before Ben can reach the plexiglass shelter. But that's okay. Walking right now is okay. He is in no hurry—his next appointment isn't for a few hours yet—and anyway, he's still a little rattled from his conversation in the fern bar. Whether his belly sizzles with anxiety over the man's story of casual violence or his backhanded admission to putting Ben in possible harm's way, walking the south-end's low and littered streets, for whatever reason, is a help. Like tracing the rust-red train tracks carving through the woods. Like the moments leading up to discovering the dragonflies swarming in a meadow. The simple act of movement is quieting. The space itself is as much a comfort as his aimless movement through it. Part of him—the part that's practiced in college-ese bullshit—wants to say it's the honesty of the neighborhood that puts him at ease—poor places don't pretend to be anything but what they are—but he knows, it's because nothing here needs him that he feels safe. Streets his students and colleagues would never walk, never drive down, perhaps don't even know exist. He's more comfortable here than he could ever be on campus. In this place, he has nothing to offer, and it asks nothing of him in return. In a few blocks, he's no longer worried about the potential of someone following him, of any menace waiting in alleyway shadows. He stops at a corner bodega and buys a donut and an orange juice. He walks his snack to the canal.

The concrete aqueduct runs parallel to a four-lane avenue with a patchy grass promenade running in between, thickly stooping Osage orange trees and basswood, black squirrels, a lone hot dog vendor eager for anyone to drop by. The cinder path alongside the canal glitters with flints of broken glass, but still, now and then bicyclists crunch past in ones and twos as Ben sits on the levee's edge, legs kicking down toward the water below. Pads of algae float on the current and beneath the surface, dark shapes move, long shadows that might very well be fish. Ben snaps open the cap of his orange juice but doesn't drink, gazes instead into the slow brackish water, his donut resting on a leaf of wax paper in his lap. Already, he is feeling better. He could sleep here, he thinks, if it ever came to that. No worse than last night's bus shelter. It's amazing the havens you can discover, he thinks, when you're trying your best to avoid home.

For a moment, he considers going to see Rubens, face the thing he's been putting off for weeks. But considering is all he does. He remains on the levee and gazes into the water, watches the dark shapes move around.

A part of Ben really would like to dismiss the man in his stupid Hawaiian shirt as a loveless goon, an undesirable, someone best kept incarcerated and safely outside the gene pool. But he knows that's a lazy way out. It's easier to demonize the grotesque than to attempt any measure of identification. And really, it doesn't take much effort for Ben to see himself reflected back. Despite the man's bravado, Ben knows there's regret seeded in his story—there's always regret, he wouldn't be telling the story otherwise—so that even when accounting for the cruelty and violence in his persona, it's undeniable the man contains a hurt, maybe many hurts, deep gashes that refuse to clot. Just like everyone else in the world. It's the bedrock over which all contours bend.

Biting into his donut, sweet glazed crumbs pebbling down his chin, Ben remembers when he first met the man less than one month ago, at the botanical gardens of all places. Rubens had just been admitted to his rehabilitation unit after months of increasingly obvious decline, barely able to light a cigarette for his shaking yellow hands, and with nothing else to do during their usual conference hour, Ben opted to go see the year's first flowers in bloom. It seemed as good an option as anything else: he always manages, no matter where he goes, to find evidence to support his thesis's claim. This was all before he was afraid to go back to his apartment, before he took to scrutinizing every shadow that crossed his path. Ben was sitting on a polished granite bench beneath the fragrant bower of a blossom-frothing cherry tree—pale petals now and then drifting down around him—and first he watched a middle-aged woman, silver streaking her waves of black hair, wandering aimlessly among a bank of pink and purple azaleas—he remembers, it looked as though she was talking to herself, smiling dreamily and holding up her end of a conversation with someone who wasn't there—and when he looked away from the azalea woman, he spotted the man in some other oversized Hawaiian shirt, absently pinching the rubbery new growth of an almost-electric-blue dwarf spruce. He was grinning dopily as he palpated the clustered needles, maybe disbelieving their unexpected supple texture, face puffy and eyes lined in red, not so much like he was hungover as still drunk from the night before. A cartoon Garfield cat-face, Ben called it at the time, dopey with overindulgence. This guy is harmless. A bumblebee thumped off the man's right shoulder, corrected its course, droned on toward the magnolias. Ben can't remember what he said to attract the man's attention, but they spoke for a moment—Ben sitting and the man standing with the garden path running in between—about all the "pretty fucking flowers" exploding absurdly into bloom. Then the man joined Ben on the bench, and beneath the gauzy April sun, he told Ben about his mentally-disabled half-brother who he hadn't seen in nearly ten years, who he'd defended throughout their childhood but now and then, apropos to nothing, he'd turn against and humiliate in public, humiliations he didn't feel the need to describe but that his brother, too simple to hold a grudge, always forgave. It wasn't a tearful confession. But it wasn't passed off as a joke either. It took nothing for Ben to coax this story from the man. It was just there, riding beneath the fuzzy haze of his hangover while his mind got blown by brand new spruce needles bursting from their buds. It's what Ben reminds himself of each time he's talked to the man since—whenever he gets the worming knot in his stomach that tells him this alliance is bad bad bad—that this self-styled gangster with all his casual talk of beatings and dirty-dealings, flexing the muscle granted by the lowest sort of power, is the same man who admitted to an old and lingering guilt he could not shake—a pedestrian sort of guilt, sure, but guilt nonetheless—for wronging someone weak who trusted him, exposing his vulnerability to a stranger in a gentle rain of cherry blossoms while yards away, the azalea woman told a joke to someone who wasn't there, laughed, then walked past them on her way to the magnolia garden, trailing in her wake a bouquet of burnt bread and crushed herbs.

Ben washes down his last bite of donut with a swig of juice while at his back, a pair of men walks past in the cinders of the canal path. He doesn't worry if they're the ones who've been following him. If anyone has, in fact, been following him. Behind him, in the promenade, there suddenly bursts the sound of young voices, laughing and shouting. Or maybe they've been there all along, swelling in volume until he cannot help but hear. Turning, Ben sees over his shoulder a group of girls in white dresses circling a flagpole rising tall and flagless near the hot dog vendor. Each holds the end of a pale pink or blue ribbon wrapping slowly around the pole, their orbit closing with each skipping step. The hot dog vendor watches in awe, hat in hand, until finally, the girls each touch the pole at their center and squealing, run away. It takes Ben a moment to register whether or not this is something he's actually seeing. He's still staring at the flagpole, ribbons coming undone on a breeze, when the faraway voices of the girls are long gone.

Turning back to the canal, Ben tells himself: what matters is this. The man was thinking contritely of his brother, but he was also looking at flowers—had intentionally sought out the Technicolor gallery of the botanical gardens—and in his own way, was happy. Just like the woman among the azaleas, laughing at her own jokes. What grief did she bear, too, that could exist side by side with glowing purple blossoms and a punch line only she could hear? It seems to Ben that he should be able to do the same thing, to adapt to the universal background radiation of his sorrow while also experiencing any fleeting joy, however it might be offered. Like Mel Goldfarb waterskiing with his family on Lake Skaneateles while quietly denying he was ever an internment camp guard. Like the mechanic indulging in some hardcore erotica while his marriage accelerated toward its inevitable end. It seems possible, if only in theory, that he could be just like them. But that buoyancy only ever finds Ben in infinitesimal, shimmering bursts when he looks *into* his grief, never past it. Like maybe if he stares into it long enough—if he can lean so close as to kiss and fall face-forward through the rarified grief holding at the center of the world—he might maybe pass through the other side.

Finishing his juice, Ben stuffs his donut's wax paper inside the bottle and winds on the orange plastic cap. No one walks behind him. No bursting laughter from the makeshift maypole. Staring into the water, he considers throwing his bottle in. Then he does. He drops the cloudy white bottle into the canal and watches it float on like a strange Lilliputian ship, rocking front to back on the water's smooth face, and for a moment he remembers Naomi's fingers lacing through the tangles of his hair on the rail bridge crossing the creek while all the bottles shattered on the rocks below, remembers her years later saying while they crossed that same creek, her voice dry and scratchy, "Awake, oh you sleepers" and not understanding what the hell she could mean while watching her toss something from her pocket—a blister-pack of gum? a foil sheet of medication?—into the water, then remembers again her saying in a hot panting whisper the one time they made love, almost like a prayer, "Lay me in peace. Raise up erect. Spread and shelter me in peace," but again, he cannot know why this comes to mind now while his empty juice bottle bobs slowly down the canal, and when it drifts through a bright patch of reflecting light—clear and white and blinding—Ben loses sight of the bottle. Then he loses sight of everything. He isn't even aware of it happening. Skidding backward through nearly twenty years: a white and measureless reflection, opening wide like a door. But what lies on the other side? More door. The door always opens to only more door. Ben hypnotizes himself on the concrete levee by gazing into the light shining off the water. For a moment, that's all he is.

It's almost four o'clock when Ben boards a bus and rides out of the south-end, gliding gently into a hypnopompic state to the engine's gruff lullaby, to the mutter of passengers, newspapers and pneumatic brakes. He wakes up in time to get off uptown at a nexus of tall buildings and taxis, people dressed smartly and walking swiftly. Skirting the crowds, Ben ducks down a narrow side street, trots to and down an intersecting avenue, then another. Arrives finally at a tall brick building, slim and straight like its neighbors down the block, books all aligned on a shelf.

A bronze plaque alongside the double doors reads THE LANGUAGE CENTERS OF THE AMERICAS. Inside—wood and stone and dim yellow light, the scent of library dust and tobacco—there's nearly no one. A woman at the front desk, bent over a book, all auburn curls and rimless glasses. In the stairwell, two Asian men conversing haltingly in Spanish. Ben climbs the three flights to the floor marked CONVERSATION LAB, steps into a long narrow room full of chatting refugees.

But this is only conjecture. Not all of these people are refugees. Ben's certain: some of them must not be refugees. Right? Yet so far, in the weeks since finding this place, each person he's conversed with shares a history of violence only partway escaped. Ben passes through the room set up so much like a library, the English students conversing together in one corner, the Spanish in another, the French at a wide table in the middle. He nods apology to the conversations he is not actually interrupting. Slips through to the back and into a smaller lounge where no one is speaking though everyone is watching, is moving. Eyes alert for any gesture, any finger's curl or snap. Ben waves hello to all the greeting hands and seats himself on a couch near the coffee machine.

It's always struck Ben as funny, how this group has

claimed this separate quiet space as its own. These people who need silence the least. Here is the woman from Nicaragua who survived when militants detonated her husband's car, living quietly on while he beside her was eviscerated by steering wheel and shrapnel and glass. Here is the Albanian girl who was raised in the hold of a drug-runner's boat, whose ears were boxed any time she made a sound, until there were no longer any sounds to be made. Here is the Sudanese orphan who, once he and his brothers made it through the wastes to Kenya, by means of a trauma either physical or psychic could no longer hear or speak. Here is the world behind the world he's always known. The world he always wished was real and now recently, maybe too late, has discovered. He sits and waits, reads the stories being exchanged—written in the air with fingers and hands, with facial expressions and swaying shoulders—until the Sarajevan comes in. Grey eyes and pale olive skin. An army jacket and cigarette-yellowed hands. He sits beside Ben on the couch for a moment, and after a few minutes of awkward signing—movements intentional and intentionally slow, for each is still tentative with this new silent tongue—Ben opens his satchel. Withdraws his tape recorder. Prepares a tape. Sets the microphone on the coffee table beside them.

This is a whole subset of his thesis: the silent interview. His transcription of the tape will be full of sound. The hiss and snap and clap of fingers and hands. The far off sound of a siren through the open window, attacking and retreating. The scratch of a pencil. Incidental vocal sounds. Ben will catalogue the sounds surrounding the interview as if they were the interview itself. Then: he will translate. In his lap, Ben opens a notebook and waits.

This man's history, Ben knows. Just a child during the siege, he was recruited by the local resistance group as a sort of child soldier. Hobbled by a broken foot (having been trampled during a sniper attack at a Red Cross medical tent), he wasn't deemed fit to carry a weapon. So they outfitted him for surveillance. A headset and a bullhorn microphone. Binoculars and a mobile radio. For among the besieged, the enemy was hidden. Or anyway, that's what everyone believed. Each day for two months, he was stationed in some other shelled-out wreck of a building. An apartment or office. Where many people had once worked and lived. Where many people had died. From here, he'd creep from window to window like a mouse between cupboards. He knew, throughout the city, there were other kids just like him. A youth army of snipers. But while they observed through the crosshairs of their scopes, he listened through the wide ear of his microphone. Spying on his neighbors. Friends and the parents of friends and his own family. Uncles and cousins. Listening and watching for any sort of plot or attack. Waiting to hear of anything worth stopping.

Mostly, it was trivial. But once, while watching people fill buckets from a water tank that a UN convoy had delivered hours earlier, a van pulled up the rubble-strewn street and drew to a halt before the thirsty crowd. Nothing more or less unusual than anything else, but there'd been rumors about car bombs, of abandoned vehicles wired to blow. No one he knew had actually seen this happen. But he knew people who knew people. Someone, somewhere, had seen a car explode. So he aimed his microphone at the van and dialed up the gain. To hear what might be transpiring within. To decipher what plot might be afoot. In this way, he had no one to blame but himself. He missed the whistling plummet of the shell. From across the river, the mortar arced and dropped and instead of the low dialogue of whispering conspirators, he heard only the scream of the van's bright bloom, a hot orange flower of shrapnel and flame. Burning tires and bodies fleeing. But he saw none of that. The sound ripped through the wires of his headphones to puncture a hole clear through his head, and the boy collapsed onto the mortar-black floor of the apartment he was spying from. Ears bleeding and body flopping in a shock-borne seizure. It was the last sound he ever heard: a mortared van two blocks away tearing through his skull.

But the man's not here to tell Ben about this. In gestures that become more fluid and natural as he signs, he tells Ben of something earlier. Before there was a war in his city. Before the violence of the world muted itself to him for good. In a brisk pidgin, Ben copies down each word he signs.

When I was a boy, he begins, *I had a friend named Ivo.* He spells out the letters of the name slowly, one at a time. Afterward, he will combine the three symbols into a single swift motion. A gesture for a name. *Ivo was my age. But I was the youngest in my family. Myself and two older brothers. Ivo was the oldest in his family. A little brother and soon a sister too. His mother and my mother were sisters. Always together. So Ivo and I were also always together. And because his little brother was an insect and my older brothers were insects, Ivo and I would play only with each other. We would hide from the others in order to play alone. We had a house we built in a tree behind his home. We threw apples and nuts at our brothers from up there. Once we found a litter of kittens on the sidewalk, and we took them to this house in the tree. Tried to raise the kittens in*—and he pauses, snapping his fingers, the word lost to him in two languages. *Like a lie but not a lie?*

A secret?

Yes, in secret. But we did not know what we were doing, and in a cold night, the kittens died. Froze or maybe did not eat enough. But my friend, he was a good friend. We were both six years old and it was summer so no school. We ran and played and collected treasures that no one else cared about. Rocks and clever-looking sticks. Toys like plastic soldiers that other kids had thrown away. No one cared what we did as long as they did not know what we did. Did not hear or see us.

But once we had a sleeping party at his house. We dressed in pajamas and ran screaming through the house and then later would share a bed but sometime in the night, I got sick so had to go home. And then later that same night, a fire started in my friend's house and everyone got out except for him. His mother and father and brother all got out of the fire, but my friend did not. My friend was not saved, though he and his brother slept in the same room. How does one brother escape from a burning bed when the other does not?

Pencil poised above the page, Ben waits for the story to go on. But the Sarajevan is done. He's looking around the room in bored anxiety: he wants a cigarette and a coffee. He needs to leave this room. So Ben shuts off the tape recorder and packs up his stuff, and together they pour burnt coffee into styrofoam cups and step out onto a fire escape. The man smokes the way some people breathe. As if it's the most natural thing to do. Like he'd die if he stopped for too long. As one is often likely to see in the city, a desiccated piece of a pigeon—just a wing, feathers and bones—rests of the fire escape grill. In a sudden and terrifying rush, too embarrassing to acknowledge even to himself, Ben wants to touch this dead thing to his mouth. He puts his nub of pencil beneath his tongue instead. With his shoe, the Sarajevan nudges the wing off the fire escape, not so much spiraling as dead falling to the alley below.

After a moment, Ben asks him what he would say if he had the chance to speak to his friend again, if there was some way to do it over, start again: what would he say? But the Sarajevan screws up his face.

Your question is for nothing. He holds his styrofoam cup between his teeth when he signs. The cigarette somehow never leaves the crook between his fingers. *What happened happened. There are no versions. None that we can know. Just the one way. What I would say to my friend is unknowable.*

But Ben knows: this man is lucky. He has been saved. Surviving the screaming violence of this world by wholly muting it. Even on a purely physical level, sound is a disruption, the agitation of once-still molecules, all vibrating to set shaking thin membranes in our heads. All sound is a violence, and these people are immune.

So Ben tells the Sarajevan about how, when he was a boy, he and his best friend once dismantled his friend's sister's boom box. *I'm not even sure why we did it*, he signs, fingers moving slowly, clumsily, still learning the movements. *We had no reason, but we took apart her radio and explored its insides. I guess we were curious to see how the thing worked. Its gears and levers and spools of wire. That's probably a big part of why he and I were friends. We were both maybe a little too concerned with why things were the way they were. We were certain we could figure it all out. So we took apart his sister's radio and put it back together and thought for sure she'd never know. But after that, all her tapes would only play in reverse.*

Across the alley, in a playground surrounded by chain-link fence, the Maypole girls are wrapping crepe around the basketball post. But even from here, Ben can see there's something wrong with their faces. These girls are not really girls. He wonders if the Sarajevan can see them, too. Lowering his hands, Ben waits, but the Sarajevan says nothing. His grey eyes seem to stare straight past Ben, across the alley and the playground and the girls who maybe were never there, through the buildings beyond to someplace where the definition of the world lies, safe and in secret. When he finally responds, his hands are like knives falling against a butcher's block.

At a high enough speed, all songs are the same played forward as in reverse. The song is the same. All songs are the same. From far enough away, any timeline is a dot. The events all occur at once. This is how the universe begins. This is also how it ends. They're the same thing. But anyway, who can hear such things now?

Pitching his cigarette over the railing, the Sarajevan

steps through the window from the fire escape back inside the conversation lab, leaving Ben to spit out the pencil he's been holding in his mouth, to scrawl in his notebook what the man has just signed. But the sound of the pencil on the page is a mortar's falling whistle. The creak of the paper a hammer's downward swing. Who can hear such things? Maybe he and Joshua ruined Naomi's radio because they were certain they wouldn't. Maybe they believed they could understand the whys of the world because all evidence proved they could not. The beginning is the end. Who can hear? It's possible the pigeon wing never rested on the grill, either. Ben escapes downstairs and back into the deepening streets.

DEAD LEAVES CAUGHT UP IN THE ROCKS, YELLOW AND ORANGE.
The fleeting memory of a scent: her mouth, her hair.
His mother's hand stroking his neck.
His father's sleeping breath.
Awake.
A few stops after Ben boards the bus, a young woman steps on—black hair swaying in a ponytail down the length her limber back—rides for two stops and gets off at the third, and Ben cannot stop watching her. Notebook forgotten in his lap (*If he hadn't gotten sick or had simply stayed the night through, would he too have died in the fire? Would his friend have survived if he'd stayed?*). Eyes watching but not really seeing. Like a voice coming muffled from another room: he almost—but not quite—has it. A strange woman enters and exits a bus, echoing an echo,

and Ben is lost.

Just blocks shy of the rehab, Ben deboards the cramped bus and at the next intersection, steps inside a corner diner shining bright against the dusk. The chrome and chipped red Formica of 1950s nostalgia, matching leather padding the stools and backing the booths lining the luncheonette's plate-glass front. The sort of place to which Ben's found himself always, as if magnetically, drawn. Almost every town in America used to have a place like this. The one in his hometown was identical though shabbier, showing its age via hues of yellow. This one, Ben thinks, seems to be doing okay. He wonders if there's a roller-towel in the bathroom. Taking a stool at the counter, he orders a cup of coffee, idly rearranges the salt and pepper and sugar shakers into patterns with the napkin tin, the tall pint of ketchup, the squat mustard jar.

Outside, the streets and sidewalks bustle with the final after-work push for home, but inside, the diner is quiet. The solo waitress—teased hair piled high and a smile that hides her bad bridgework—sets down Ben's coffee and a menu without so much as a hiya. The cook is just a shifting shape barely visible through the square porthole into the kitchen. No music. The low sizzle of something on the grill. The only other customer is a middle-aged man—blonde mohair coat and the thick fleshy build of a longhorn bull—gazing placidly through his smudged eyeglasses at a newspaper inexpertly pulled apart, pouring all over his end of the counter.

Ben doesn't need to taste his coffee to know it's nothing he wants, and though the scent of bacon and fries and milkshakes is pleasing, it's not pleasing enough to make him hungry. He knows, he should just walk the last couple blocks to Rubens. And it's exactly that—the *should*, the force of obligation—that keeps Ben fixed to his stool. He doesn't want to go, doesn't want to see what he knows he'll see there, face what he knows he'll face. Between going home and going to see Rubens, Ben will gladly accept any other offer at hand. Nursing a cup of warmed-over coffee is as good an alternative as anything else.

Pouring half-and-half from a plastic thimble into his cup, Ben watches the white ribbon dissolve into the black. Sees his reflection pushed back against the surface. Sees the Sarajevan, styrofoam cup clamped between his teeth. Steady grey eyes. Snapping hands. Through all his interviews with the sign language group—the Sarajevan and Nicaraguan, the too-thin Albanian girl, the Buddha-cheeked Sudanese boy—it's struck Ben that nearly all of them have suffered punishments intended for someone else, each one an innocent casualty at the edges of some greater, uglier conflict that had no reason to involve them. Many of them were just children, a fact that clearly afforded them exactly zero mercy. And while Ben might feel like their muting of the world is a sort of gift, not one of them sees their deafness in such beneficent light. They miss music. They miss the sound of laughter. It's not anything they'll likely get back. And the memory of someone's voice—someone who loves you saying something important, something you want to hear—is probably cold comfort compared to the silence than drones on and on. It all seems so needlessly cruel, to punish people—to scar their bodies and plunge them in silence—for no other reason than they were there for it to happen.

But, as the Sarajevan said, there are no versions of the world. None that we can see, anyway. There might be infinite parallel universes where none of these deafening, world-shattering events took place. But not for us. Those happy lives belong to someone else. The evidence shows, the only possible outcome is the outcome that exists. Which makes a pretty strong argument that all these things were meant to be. Each moment perfect because each moment's unique. The exploding car perfect. The burning house perfect. The silenced world perfect.

Staring into his coffee, Ben feels this logic is sound. But it doesn't make him feel any better about heading down the street to see Rubens in his rehab. Or about the eventuality of going home. Or anything else, for that matter.

At the counter's end, the waitress comes with a glass of milk and a bacon cheese burger on a small blue plate, sets them each down before the man gathering up his mess of newspapers. He thanks the waitress and squares himself over his plate, and it's with incredible patience and devotion that he takes and chews his first solemn bite—from his end of the counter, Ben can hear his long deep breath drawn slowly through his nose—eyes inclined toward the ceiling lights in an almost religious sort of concentration.

Ben watches the man eat for a few minutes before he speaks.

"You'll have to forgive me for interrupting," Ben says,

"but by the look on your face, I'm guessing that's got to be the best damn burger any man has ever eaten. Am I right?"

Wide-set eyes flicking toward Ben through the lenses of his clouded glasses, the man laughs around his mouthful—napkin pressed to his lips—and nods an emphatic yes. In this gesture, Ben sees clearly this man as a little boy. Thick, bespectacled, enjoying his food. The two look exactly alike.

"It is a good burger," the man declares when he swallows.

"From my vantage? It looked like you were searching for just the right words to propose marriage to the thing."

Again, the man laughs, a healthy, chest-filling sound. "Oh, I would, too. If I weren't already spoken for, I'd—" He drinks from his milk and wipes his mouth, forgets what he was about to say. Works the napkin in his hand a minute. Stares abstracted at his plate. Outside, a fire truck whooshes down the street, its undercarriage chains clinking against the pavement. Whatever he's remembering, Ben thinks, it's making him happy. The man turns his plate a needless quarter turn. Then he slides his dinner down the counter and takes a stool nearer Ben, leaving a single empty seat between them. As if waiting for another late party to arrive.

"Used to be a time," the man says, clearing his throat, "that I'd luncheon now and then with my little—, well. I sometimes liked calling him my Serious Young Scholar. Or, when we were both feeling a little pedantic, I'd call him the Hasid."

"The hayseed? Was that some facetious opposites thing? Like a fat guy named Tiny?"

"No," and he draws out the syllable, twisting his mouth as

if a little bit embarrassed: "He was a very studious Jewish kid."

And for no reason he can name, Ben is suddenly beaming.

"Hey, I had a Jewish friend growing up."

Almost instantly, he feels like a boob.

Maintaining a patient, fool-suffering smile, the man dismisses the interruption with a blink. "Good for you. But this Serious Young Scholar of mine, he was strict, right, adhering to all the dietary rules and what have you, but he was also curious, incorrigibly so, about just about everything. He didn't like there to be unknowns in his life, especially when the knowledge was so handy. And what could be easier than washing down a beef frank with a tall glass of milk, right? So. What our lunchtime game became was, I would explain to him *what it was like* to eat these, uh, untouchable foods. What's the word the philosophers use? Phenomenology? Our lunches together turned into an exercise in phenomenology. Am I using that word right?"

"Not really, but it's close enough."

"Truth is, all my philosophy comes to me filtered through my kids, so close enough's the best I'll ever get. But what I mean is, I was trying to transfer to my Serious Young Scholar my experience of a plate of bacon or a shrimp cocktail or whatever. A cheese steak. And not just the taste either, mind you, we were going for the full shebang. The way the food melted or crunched, if it tickled the back of your throat, the way all the parts of, say, a BLT worked together to achieve something very different from the individual ingredients on their own. You know what I mean?"

"Sure. You were his surrogate mouth."

Snapping his fingers, the man points at Ben.

"Yes, exactly. I experienced for him everything he couldn't experience on his own."

"Did it work?"

"Oh. Of course not. That's the whole point when these guys talk about phenomenology. You can't know what it's like to be anyone but you. And even that's maybe a suspect claim. You can work really hard at *imagining* what it's like and *pretend* to be someone or something else—a bat or your lunch buddy or some ash piled up under your Webber grill—but pretending is as close as you'll get. It's still you being you, pretending you're something you're not."

Somehow, this feels like a belly flop. It makes Ben's insides hurt.

"Kinda sucks the romance out of empathy, huh?"

The man waves one hand through the air as if clearing a bad odor.

"Who needs romance. I think it's good practice nonetheless. What's the harm in trying to imagine what someone else's experience is like? Worst case scenario: you get it wrong. And you know, whether or not I ever gave a good, clear idea of what eating a ham and cheese was really like, it was a fun game for the kid and me to play. It taught me, if nothing else, to enjoy my food on a much more conscious level. And it made our lunches special."

"So that's what you were doing just now, right?"

"Mm-hmm. Exactly." Revolving his stool, the man looks out through the plate-glass windows onto the evening street, as if there's something out there he means to see. "I dilly-dallied too long after meeting with a client and missed my train back home. Distracted by a toy store.” Reaching into his pocket, the man sets a wind-up monkey on the counter. “I got this for my wife.” The monkey’s wearing a fez and clasping a pair of cymbals. The man winds it and sets it marching across the Formica, then stashes it back in his pocket, still buzzing and whacking away. “I figure, as long as I’ve got to wait for my next caboose home, I might was well enjoy the old game. Remember my little buddy. Take detailed notes on the forbidden.” Turning back to the counter, he appraises almost gravely his plate. “Beef and pig with cheese and milk. Add a couple crab legs, and you’re about as far from matzoh as you can get.”

Ben gives an unsure laugh. The man only manages a commiserating grin. Already, the mood has changed. In an automatic gesture, they each take a drink. The coffee, Ben notices, has not much improved by cooling.

“So your friend—”

“We don’t talk the way we used to.” And he grins, still watching his plate, silver shining in the faint stubble on his cheeks. “No hard feelings.”

Coming in from the kitchen, the waitress makes a production of emptying the coffee pots, bangs the carafes in the sink. So much for a warm-up. Ben can’t tell if he agrees with the man or not. The unspannable distance between any two people. Playing a philosophical game with a friend who’s long gone. He doesn’t know how he feels about this. Other than it sounds familiar. Looking down at the Marantz tilted against the stool’s chrome post, Ben wonders if he should ask. But the man beats him to it.

“So what’s that, your sample case or something?” He

speaks with a bite of burger tucked into his cheek. "Selling vitamins and carpet samples door to door?"

"Do people still do that sort of thing?"

"I hope not. For their own sake."

"Right. No, no vitamins. I'm involved in a documentary project." And he taps the Marantz with the toe of one shoe. "It's a tape recorder."

"Hmm." He's chewing more than listening now. "What's your project about?"

"Mostly it's just these couple of questions I like to ask. People tend to fill the gaps in on their own, if that makes sense."

"Sure, sure." The man's nodding, wiping his lips. "Alright." His five o'clock shadow makes confetti of his napkin. "Let's see it." His burger, half eaten, splays across his plate. "Ask away."

"You'd like to—?"

"Yeah, yeah, bring it out." And he claps his hand as if they were dusty. "We'll see if I can take the scrutiny."

On the dry-erase board mounted high up on the wall, surrounding the day's specials—meatloaf sandwich, bratwurst and onions, and, simply put, cake—someone has drawn a cascade of flowers, plain daisies in pink and blue. Through the kitchen porthole underneath, the cook isn't even pretending not to stare. Ben meets his eyes as he fishes his satchel from the floor. Let him stare.

From the stool beside him, the man with the burger watches bemused while Ben sets up the Marantz—plugs in the microphone, installs a fresh tape—working his tongue around in his mouth, sucking clean his teeth. By the time

Ben hits RECORD and tests the levels, the man seems composed if not also entertained.

"Would you mind stating your name for the tape?"

Smiling a tight-lipped near-frown, he shakes his head no.

"Okay. No name. Well. We started off talking about your strictly curious—what'd you call him, your Serious Young Scholar?—so maybe, continuing along that same line of inquiry, you'd like to tell me about your best friend?" And after a beat: "It doesn't necessarily have to be your hayseed friend."

Before the man can speak, the waitress comes around to drop off their checks, giving the recording setup a stern once-over. Both Ben and the man tell her thank you when she leaves.

"You know, it's funny. Everyone always talks about their best friends. Especially when they're young. Everyone's got a best friend when they're young. Men more than women, I've noticed. But I don't think I ever did that. I never pinpointed one person and said, 'You, you are the best of my affections.' Not until I met my wife, anyway, though I suspect that's something different. Though maybe not? I mean, until I had a family, I seriously never thought of other people as my friends, let alone *best* friends. They were all just people, the whole world just chockablock full of people, and while I might like some, none of them were my friends. Until I had a family. Then my family was my friend."

"Your family—"

"Yep. Been married over thirty years. The wife's a part-time piano and voice instructor at the school and a full-time letter writer at home. Though it beats me who she's writing to. Probably one of our two perfect kids." And he smiles, as if the joke is for him alone. "One more consistently perfect than the other."

"Care to elaborate on that?"

"Not at all."

"I figured as much. So you're all pretty close."

"Well, as close as anyone can be to anyone else." And before Ben can ask: "It's the phenomenology thing again. Your relationship to a person isn't about the person, it's about your *ideas* surrounding that person. They don't even need to be present, in the strictest sense of the word. In fact, it's sometimes better if they're not. Or anyway, it's easier. They can't contradict your idea of them that way. But yeah, I like the *idea* of my wife and kids a lot, much more than I like the idea of anyone else I've ever met. So I guess they're my best friends."

"Whether they're around or not."

"Especially when they're not." Against the plate-glass: the night's first hard splatters of rain. "I'd be lonely without them when they're away somewhere else."

From the kitchen, the cook rings his bell. But there is no order up.

"I think I know what you mean," Ben says, "but that sounds a little confusing."

"Try memorizing a hamburger sometime. That'll clear your mind like nothing else."

But to that, Ben's got nothing to say. Through the porthole into the kitchen: the cook is gone.

"Alright. Well. I usually ask folks about their thoughts

on second chances, what they think of that possibility, what they'd do if they were given a particular second chance." Pausing, Ben worries his tongue among his teeth. As if he's the one who's been eating. "But I get the feeling you don't go in for that sort of thing."

"Yeah. No. You see, that sort of thinking, to me, that's all about regret. It's backward-thinking."

"And you're forward-thinking, right?"

"Mm, well, if my wife were here? She'd tell you I'm *anti*-thinking. Her opinion is that I'm not engaged in the world, that I don't feel things deeply enough. And maybe I don't. It's possible I'm not engaged in the world. But I don't think so. Like, say you're describing a thing, a chair or a cat or some flowers in a bottle, and you use certain words, and the people listening, as a consequence, feel a certain way about the thing. Now let's say you describe that same cat or flower or whatever with different words—all synonyms of the first words, you know, so the meaning is the same—and people will have a different understanding of that thing. Calling the sky azure instead of blue. You're framing the world in a different way. And my framing, I guess, is quieter than my wife's. Quiet enough so she can claim it maybe isn't even there."

Changing the world just by changing your words. This, again, Ben can't unpack enough to know whether he agrees.

"So. Not forward- or backward-thinking. Just… *quiet*-thinking. Letting the world happen without my dictating what it's all supposed to mean. That might be disengagement after all. But one thing I'm certainly *not* engaged with, getting back to your question, is beating myself up over things that've passed and can't possibly be changed. I can't see a point in feeling bad when I don't need to. I'm just not concerned with it." It suddenly occurs to Ben: they want to close. The dumped out carafes. The cook ringing the bell. It's past time they should leave. "I mean, look, you can spend your whole life wishing the bad things in your past never took place, and you can make all kinds of plans and strategies to guarantee that those kinds of hurt never happen again, but between the one sort of worrying and the other, there's no room left for you to live your life. It's a systematic full-time distraction, one that won't ever allow you the chance to notice something so joyfully banal as whether or not your lunch was any good, if it even tasted like anything. It sounds simplistic, sure, but I can't really see any other viable option. If my choice is between regret and a hamburger, I choose the hamburger every time."

And as if to prove his point, the man gathers up his fallen-apart dinner and takes an enormous bite. Watching him chew, Ben pushes the muscles of his face into a smile. But he suspects it doesn't pass.

"That's a very different answer," he says, "than what I'm used to hearing from people." A statistical outlier. Something to disregard. Already, he's making plans to throw this tape away.

Twirling the milk in his glass, the man says before taking a sip, "Which means it's probably the answer you need to hear." Swallowing, he sets down the glass with a wet *thunk* against the Formica. "But! In my experience, these kinds of questions? They tell more about the person asking than the person answering. Know what I mean?" Picking up his napkin, he laves it between his hands, tosses it balled up onto his plate. Something disarmingly familiar gleams in his animal eyes. "So the real question *now* becomes, what regretful thing do *you* wish you had a second chance at?" And leaning in closer, his laughing eyes catch Ben's startled eyes. "Perhaps *you*, my Serious Young Scholar, should tell me about *your* best friend."

Ben's mouth falls open. But he doesn't speak a sound. The cook in the kitchen pours seltzer on the grill to deglaze the day's browned fat. The waitress wipes down a booth. Outside, May's first rain sizzles on the pavement. He's waiting. Raising one hand, Ben extends a finger. He presses the button marked STOP.

IT SEEMS FROM AN AGE BEFORE KINDNESS. ALL SHARP LINES and brick and iron. A clever trick of forging wire into the window glass. Past the heavy double set of double doors, Ben is told by a security guard that the stairs are broken, that he'll have to take the elevator. As the metal cage rattles up to the fifth floor, Ben has time to reflect on why he's never come here before.

The floor Ben arrives on is a minor maze, rooms with closed doors and rooms whose doors are open but reveal nothing. Empty beds and naked IVs. There's a room like a cafeteria and a window in a wall where maybe pills are dispensed. But there's no one there now. Ben wanders lost and turned around until he finds his mentor by accident in some sort of game room—a TV mutely playing a Western soap-opera rerun, a ping-pong table green as a walnut hull, a chess game half-played and abandoned—propped in a wheelchair by the window, watching the night rain lash the glass.

Everything here looks jaundiced. Ben pulls a yellow chair across the yellow linoleum, sits halfway facing Dr. Rubens by the window. Sets his briefcase on the floor and the satchel in his lap. Then, for a while, he just holds the Marantz. Feels its leather creak beneath his thumbs. Its weight against his thighs a solid comfort. After his talk with the man in the diner, another interview seems like a bad route to follow. Yet the alternative—straight talking without the shielding buffer of a microphone—somehow seems much worse. The tape of the man with the dirty eyeglasses rests where he left it in the machine. Ben peels open the satchel's flap and hits REWIND. Plugs in the microphone and props it on the windowsill. Checks the levels and checks the tape. Sets the Marantz to RECORD. Makes his last interview disappear. One spooled second at a time.

"They won't let me smoke in here," is what his mentor finally says. "Do you know that?" Rubens' hair was once deep brown but has recently thinned and grown shot-through with grey. Skin loose as Ben's ill-fitting clothes. "Others can smoke. So it's not a policy thing." His voice is a mucousy rumble. "I am disallowed for reasons obscure, Ben. And all I want is a cigarette."

A nurse walks down the hall and through the room, past both men and out another hall. She makes no effort to address them in her passing. But she is all cat-eyes as she goes.

"It's hard to say goodbye after your love is gone."

Rubens looks away from the window for the first time, considers the microphone, gestures vaguely with a limp finger.

"So am I to be a part of this now? Another entry in your catalog? You know this is a conflict of interests, right?" He does not look at Ben. He stares at the microphone and the rain-streaked window beyond. "They call this a rehab, Ben, but it's a wake. Is that too maudlin? It *is* too maudlin. We've all been invited to our own funereal viewing. Tell me how that's not maudlin. They call it a cancer ward when they think no one can hear, but I hear, Ben, and no, it's not even that. It's a prison wearing the linens of a tomb."

A long silent moment passes. In his transcripts, Ben will note its length. As if it, too, were part of the interview. The silence being the most telling part. He can wait forever. Most people, however, cannot. Eventually, Rubens tells Ben of a time in the 1970s when he worked as a merchant marine. To see the world slowly and at a low cost. To achieve an amount of quiet in his life. To see who he might be outside the context of everything that he was.

"I read a lot of books at sea and paid for the clap more than once when in port. I turned out to be just as uninteresting as any other young man in my position."

On one stint, he was part of a crew delivering turbines that would be used by some equatorial government in constructing offshore windmills. "There was a crisis. No way to power anything. Everyone was looking for alternatives." They delivered the massive turbines to an island swamp a mile from the mainland. The constructing engineers had almost no staging area, just the merchant ship and countless pylons jammed into the reef beneath them. Because there was no other place to go with them, each turbine had to be installed as soon as the crane lifted it off the deck. So they unloaded their cargo one piece at a time. "We were stranded at sea for days with little to nothing to do. So of course someone would eventually find the manatees."

To their credit, the manatees weren't eager to not be found. Friendly, curious creatures, milling in the waters surrounding the working ships, by all appearances enthralled and watching the human business at hand. "They were so easy to shoot that it seemed foolish not to." So the crew began taking shots at the pale, swimming cows. Never too many at once. Often just one or two a day. "A lot of the guys had their own pistols they'd brought or bartered for at port, but you know, those ships are lousy with flare guns. Anyone could have a turn." By the time the last turbine was installed and the ship's engines roared awake to bear them back to the north, the bodies were everywhere. Floating and reeking. Fodder for sharks and for birds.

"To everyone else, it was a game, but I couldn't get it. We were building windmills at sea. We were killing beautiful animals too simple to know to be afraid."

Rubens closes his eyes and pinches his nose's bridge. Wipes his mouth, then his whole lower face. Rubs fiercely at his eyes. Tugs the end of his thinning hair.

"So how's that, Ben? A young man watching animals die and never once speaking up to stop it. Knowing that speaking up wouldn't've have changed a thing. Feeling guilty for it all the same. Is that the sort of thing you came here for? Something to hold up heroically against yourself?”

For as long as he can, Ben lets the silence hold. Then slowly, leaning forward, he withdraws from his back pocket a folded sheet of paper—deeply creased and bent into the shape of his hip—opens and lays it across his mentor’s knee.

“I need you to sign this.” It escapes neither’s notice that this is the first thing he’s said since arriving. “It states that you’ll allow someone else to review my work. Dr. Mulholland has already agreed to step in even this late in the game. It’s my only chance of having my thesis heard.”

Rubens stares at the paper in his lap. But he makes no move to touch it.

“Your thesis.” He drawls the words long and low in his throat. As if they tasted bad. “And what exactly is your thesis supposed to be, Ben?”

All day, he’s felt this coming.

“C’mon, Rubens, don’t fuck with me here.”

Water building above the dam. Eyes suddenly bright, Rubens claps his hands.

“Ah, I’m fucking with you, am I?”

“Yes, you’re fucking with me. You’re—”

Like there’s a distance between himself and his own spitting words.

“It’s so exciting to see your sallow blood pumping, Nigra, it really is.”

“Goddamnit, you know—”

“Do I know? I don’t think I do, Ben. I honestly can’t understand what it is you’re trying to prove. Look at yourself. You sleepless bug-eyed creep. You’re scraping up every single sob story you can find about so-and-so missing their sweet precious what's-his-name, about how they should've done X when instead they did Y. And what does it all reveal? That life's one long harsh toke? That no one ever has exactly *nothing* left to lose?"

He can feel his fingernails biting into his palms. But already, his anger is spent. Opening his hands, Ben looks down at the cassette's turning spindle, winding down the tape, the microphone on the sill and the rain on the glass, anywhere but at his mentor.

"You're going to have to do a lot better than that, Ben," Rubens says, stabbing with his finger the form laid across his lap, "if you want me to sign this paper. You'll have to do way better in your defense."

Far down one of the hallways sounds the echoed rattle of something like a tin pail falling on the floor, followed by a long, plaintive "oh." Neither one of them turns to look.

"Right before I came over here," Ben says, "I'm pretty sure I interviewed myself. The only difference was, this guy loved all the things in him that I hate about me."

Rubens turns over his hands, claps them back onto his armrests.

"What is that, some Zen bullshit? A koan for me to think deeply upon? Quit fucking around, Nigra. You've got a point to all you're doing? Then spit it out."

The most amazing part of it all, he thinks, is that he's missed these conversations. Closing his eyes, Ben sees the light shining white off the hallway floor. The needle whispering over his mother's turning record. The limbs of the mantis articulating behind Mason glass. A thing he can't name falling to the water from Naomi's open hand.

"Sometimes," he says, "our grief can be a weapon. And sometimes it can be a tool." He opens his eyes and meets his mentor's eyes. "It can also be a noose."

"That sounds more like a threat than a thesis, Ben."

"It is threatening." And he looks away. "But not in the way you mean."

A long moment passes before either one of them speaks again. The whirring of the cassette. Rain whacking against the glass. "You're snowballing me." Sighing, Rubens turns the sheet over in his lap, as if something might be revealed in its blank white underside. "But you're snowballing yourself even more." Leaning forward in his wheelchair, Rubens looks Ben square in the eyes: he has to snap his fingers to make sure it happens. "I'll consider signing this." He folds the paper and slips it into the pocket of his yellow robe. "But know that I won't. I won't sign it." And it's gone. "How better to make real a treatise on loss than to lose that as well. Am I right?"

Behind them, a man with a nasal cannula leads himself into the room, green and grey oxygen tank wheeling behind his left hand. His features tiny within the bulk of his body. His breath a hiss and a rattle and a wheeze. He lowers himself eternally into a chair by the TV. He groans when his weight is finally allowed to release.

"I know you can't see it this way," Rubens rasps, "but I am helping you. You're making a mistake and refuse to see it. This is for your own good."

Think quietly. Change the world by changing your words. Ben turns off the recorder and packs his microphone, touches Rubens' shoulder as he stands to leave. Beneath his robe: the feel of thin bones. He cannot picture his mentor as a child. He can't even picture him before he was sick.

"You're getting what you deserve, you know."

"So are you."

In the hospital's entryway, between the twin sets of doors, Ben stops to find in his briefcase a duplicate of the form. Draws a line down the middle of his tongue with the tip of a black ink pen. Forges his mentor's name. As he's always had to forge his mentor's name.

AS A TEENAGER, BEN WOULD WANDER THROUGH THE WOODS and meadows outside of town, aiming himself in no particular direction while wading among tall grass and briar, beneath the nodding boughs of poplar and ash, the motion reducing his body into a simple, unthinking machine. An unguided vehicle roaming through the world. It calmed him. It made him feel less alone. Leaving the dingy austerity of Rubens' hospital, Ben finds himself engaging again this very same technique. He wanders the night streets in a blind and idiot daze. He does not acknowledge that he's thinking. He does not acknowledge what he feels. The rains have stopped but the fog has returned, turning every streetlight into hazy will-o'-the-wisps, making every street sign foreign and obscure. Everything indistinct and alien in the fog: it barely registers when he passes into the city's China Town. He does not see the pictograph signs or epicanthic eyes. He stands for a while outside the plate glass of a butcher's shop, gazing unseeing at the glistening meats. The inflated ducks. The spools of sausage. It's the shiny whole suckling pigs, each roped and strung up by its fetlocks, that snap him back to the present. All their perfect cleft hooves. Perhaps just barely twitching in the fog light. Impossibly alive. Impossibly not. For the second time today, he wants to touch something dead to his mouth.

He decides he is being followed. Then he decides he's not.

But there are only so many ways to make another night go away. Eventually, Ben dips into a Korean bar with karaoke and soju, drinks two glasses of cold rice wine while a group of young men attempts one awful rendition after another of "I Will Always Love You," and after they've each tried his best, Ben settles up and drifts again through foggy streets, past pho houses and sushi bars, out of China Town and into a working-class neighborhood where he spots a country pub glowing beneath a neon Narragansett sign. Nurses a beer while watching two women in matching cowboy hats try and fail to get a line dance going. Instead of leather boots, one of the women boasts a pair of hooves. It almost doesn't bother him. Of course the goblins love line music. Of course the goblins are here. He moves along. He stops at a dive bar and a leather bar and a Sonoran bar where everything seems glazed in *aguardiente*, and eventually Ben winds up at a sprawling dance club and lounge, its cavernous dark warm and crowded with people shouting and laughing, moving to the music pouring through the PA—the constant deep *whump* of bass and the occasional contrail of a glow-stick slashing past—and without meaning or intention, Ben finds himself hovering by the Lucite bar in a bouquet of flavored vodka and in mid-conversation with a young man whose face keeps swimming in and out of focus. As if the night's fog has crept in like a stray cat through a window. He's not entirely certain how he got here. There were bodies and strobelights and the almost merciless throb of music. Then there was this guy, seemingly eager to talk: he's got something important to say. Ben reaches for his tape recorder, but the kid just waves it away.

"Look, I wanna—"

"You can't. You can't use any of this, man. It isn't yours to have."

Things sharpen. Things diminish. He doesn't know when he got so drunk.

"But—"

"All you'd get on tape is Daft Punk anyway."

The young man considers the beer in his glass before continuing.

"What I was trying to say though is, before all this, I never really knew my dad. I mean, he's always been around, it's not like he took off when I was a kid or anything. We talk and do things together. But now, I don't know. It's like he's a real person."

Not a real person. *Like* a real person. Ben weaves closer to the speaking figure, weaves away.

"Like, there was this one time. He'd've been about my age now, and this cousin of his dies. My dad's going to school in Indiana, but the funeral's in Ohio. I mean, the whole family is in Ohio. So my dad's kind of stranded, right? No way to get there. But his roommate lends Dad his car, and Dad goes to the funeral. Drives all night and gets there just in time. And it's like, you know, the *getting there* became the hard thing for him, right? For everyone else, the funeral is the challenge. The grief and loss and shit, seeing the body all laid out then closed up and paraded around. But Dad had already met his challenge. He got there and saw his cousin into the ground and was able to comfort his aunt and uncle and their surviving children, you know, his other cousins. He was kind of like the anchor bolt holding the family together, if only for that one day.

"But you know, the next morning comes, obviously, and he has to drive his friend's car back to Indiana, and it's somewhere along the way that the transmission goes. Just like that. He remembers seeing a garage a little ways back along whatever little stretch of highway he's on, so he walks back and the mechanic agrees to tow and fix the car, but he says it'll take a few days to get all the parts and get it all together, and it's going to cost all this money, and you know, there's my dad. Out in the middle of some wheat field somewhere with no money and his grief on pause and he's stranded. He may as well've been naked in a desert in Mongolia or something, some fucking island somewhere. And that's what I keep thinking about. My dad before he was my dad, marooned on a highway surrounded by nothing but wheat and sky and it fucking kills me every time."

A moment passes to the music and laughter and the clinking of glasses off glasses. Ben can see this kid's father standing pointlessly on the tarmac, an anonymous monument among sun and wind and the sound of swishing grain. Ben sees his own father flip the record, reset the needle.

"You know, both my folks—"

But the kid waves him off. "I know, Mr. Nigra, I know. You don't have to talk about it if you don't want to."

The lens tips, slips out of focus.

"How do you—? How can you know my—?"

The lens tips back.

"You're kidding, right? Something like that? The whole department knows."

The cheeks and eyes. The inadvertent smirk. The details coalesce into the flattop junior, his most prized and most loathed student, and again Ben is washed in the sick vertigo of being lost, but the kid doesn't care—he's been forgotten before—buys Ben a drink and leads him from the bar to a table in the corner where a half-dozen or so of his other students are assembled, drinking and laughing and gathered to tell their stories, the histories they've uncovered, the spare bits and pieces of their lives and parents' lives and grandparents' lives that cannot fit into their final reports. The cherished details they must give up. The things lost once and lost again.

They have a name for this game. They call it "shooting the puppy."

"Back after the First World War," says the girl with the dangerous mouth and long blonde braid, "there were these limits on who could enter this country, fucking quotas. So many Polacks. So many Italians. On some of the boats coming over, there were limits, too. Quotas on quotas, right? They'd only let so many members of any given family on board. Which was fine by my great-grand-parents. It was just the two of them. Soon it'd be three, but when they booked their voyage, yeah, just two. Their first baby would be born in America, be born American, hurray. Except my great-grandmother went into labor early, like two months early, it's two or three days before they're supposed to get the hell out of Germany and suddenly they've got a little baby girl. Whoops! How's that going to work? My great-grandmother's freaking out, but my great-grandfather, he stays calm, tells her it'll be okay, and he goes out and finds a shoebox. Right? They pack my infant grandmother in a little shoebox and sneak her onto the boat like luggage. Once the boat was moving, of course, it was fine. It wasn't like they kept her in there the whole time. But still: my grandmother crossed the Atlantic in a shoebox. Slipped through Ellis Island in a shoebox. All official documentation states she was born in New York City two days after my great-grandparents arrived. Fucking A, right?"

They all applaud at the end of her story. As they applaud the end of each story. They welcome it into the world. They bid it graciously farewell.

"My father lived on the border during the war between Egypt and Israel," tells the deep-brown boy with short dreadlocks and lover's eyes. "He was just a little guy when the fighting started, maybe five or six years old. But his family lived way up in the hills, far away from any town or even any real roads, so no one was worried. The war couldn't possibly find them up there and anyway, why would anyone want to bother with them? Honestly, he doesn't even remember anyone even talking about the war. It was just something he figured out later, when he had time to piece it all together. And anyway, way up in the hills like that? It could be they didn't even know. It was only a week long war.

"Anyway, there was this one day when he was up on a hill with the family's little goatherd, right, and while he's standing up there with the animals, he sees this whole battalion of soldiers come pouring over the opposite ridge into the valley where his family's farm was. I mean, they didn't even slow down or stop or anything, just swallowed up the farm and set everything on fire and continued through the canyon on their way to wherever. And my father, he just stands there. What fucking else can he do? This isn't like anything he ever heard of or even dreamed about, you know, had nightmares about. So he stands there and watches them come and go and then watches the farm burn for a long time, then finally he leaves the goats behind to investigate, and you know, I can see it. I can see this little boy walking between burning buildings, calling out for his mom or dad or sisters. But you know no one's going to answer. There's no one *left* to answer. So my dad wanders around for a few days, not knowing what to do. I mean, he's just a kid. He follows the goats for a while, but they eventually lose him. So then he wanders alone. By the time anyone found him, it was days later and the war was over and the border had changed and here's this little war orphan who has no idea if he's Jewish or Muslim, Egyptian or Israeli. He was too young to know what he was."

"What happened to him then?" asks the flattop.

"I mean, what the hell happens to a war orphan in the Middle East?" But why is Ben playing this game, insisting on unnaming the named. The blonde girl is Gretchen. The lover's eyes belong to Jean-Paul. Nancy and Kevin and Calder and Meghan are all waiting and listening and watching, and Bret is asking about the fate of Jean-Paul's orphan father.

"He was found on the Israeli side, so he was taken in by an Israeli family. Oddly enough—or is it odd?—the only language my father spoke then was French. So maybe he rightfully belonged to neither country. But all his life, he's been suspicious that he was maybe Egyptian, maybe Muslim. And he knows, if he'd been found on the other side of the border, his suspicions would reverse. It's like he *can't* know who he's supposed to be."

"So what nationality does your family claim?" Meghan's kohl-painted eyes and the stud through her lip gleam in the neon bar light.

"Well, we're Americans, you know? I was born in LA. But my mother's family is from Lebanon. So she and I indentify at least a little bit as Lebanese. But my father claims nothing. He says his name is label enough."

With ritualistic patience, one by one, his students share their private histories—the missing parents, the lost branches of the family—each performing the incantation that Ben has been teaching them, this simple act of necromancy: bringing back from the dead these people and places lost to us. This summoning of voice. The grateful banishment of clapping hands. When finally his turn comes, when he balks and they egg him on, their smiles and eyes and voices all invitations,

Ben briefly forgets who he is. For one moment, he feels a part of something. So he speaks of his fleeting experience, the ghost of having once been a part.

"This isn't a family thing, not really. I don't want to talk about that. But when I was a little boy, I had a very close friend who died. We were maybe eight or nine and he died very suddenly. He was the only friend I had. So for a long time after that, I had no friends at all. Seriously. I just shut down. I had a cousin I was close with, but she lived a long ways away. So except for the times when she visited, I was a robot. I did what was expected of me at home and at school. Beyond that, though, I did not engage.

"But at some point in high school, I became close with my dead friend's sister. She was older by a couple years and there was something about her that—even when we were kids, I remember thinking something about Naomi was powerful. Like a switchblade. Not dangerous or violent or anything. Just very…intentional. She was efficiently designed for a purpose. I was hypnotized by that. And too, maybe more than anything else, she was the only person who understood what my loss was like. She and I would go out and get high in the same stretch of woods that her brother and I used to play in, you know, sit with our feet in the creek or lie on our backs in the tall grass. The sort of shit kids do in a Linklater movie. Except all we would talk about was my dead friend. How everything he saw in the world was either a tremendous joke or evidence of the divine. We both knew things about him that the other could never have known. So we each got to discover Joshua all over again. It was almost like having him back.

It seriously felt like we could keep him alive somehow if we kept talking about him. Like we could somehow save him and make things right." Ben laughs quietly to himself and wipes his face, his brow and his eyes. "She and I slept together one time. I guess that was the culmination of the thing. It was my first time but not hers. Her folks were gone and she brought me into her room but really, it was my friend's old room. She'd moved into her brother's old room and changed nothing. Absolutely nothing. A seventeen-year-old girl living in a nine-year-old boy's room. And it was only then that it hit me that her grief and her loss were so much bigger than mine. Mine just existed in my head, you know. Hers was a three-dimensional space. It contained her. She was living every second in his memory. Even his glow-in-the-dark stars were still glued to the ceiling. And that's where she took my virginity. In my friend's old bed. Beneath the constellations he invented. And man, I gladly gave myself to her. And not in the way that every teenage boy gratefully gives himself to the first girl who'll have him. As naïve as it sounds, I really believed we could make him real again this way. It was some forgotten Earth magic. I remember thinking that. We were calling him back. Right where he used to sleep and breathe. We could bring him back."

In the liquid dark of the bar, between flashes of the strobes, he can see her. Not as she was in her brother's bed. He sees her hand opening to drop something in the water, letting go of something he cannot see well enough to name, while she tells him in her own way: *wake up!*

"But. You know. That obviously was not going to happen.

A girl as smart as she was wasn't about to get knocked up by her dead brother's best friend. She made me pull out. That's probably more information than you guys wanted. At the very moment I thought it was happening, that we'd done it, she sprung off of me and I came in her mouth. Which struck me as the very opposite of what I thought we were trying to do. Not so much a séance as a door slamming shut. And after that, she wouldn't even talk to me. I know there was a lot going on then that I wasn't aware of, and too, it probably wasn't good for her to be hanging out with me. Just my being around probably undid a lot of the work she must've had to do for herself. But still. It felt like a rejection. Or really, like an amputation. I was an extra limb she didn't need. She made me gone. And eventually she graduated and moved away. Which I guess meant both of us were gone."

He sees her hand open. He sees her letting go.

"Do you know where she is now?" someone asks, but Ben can't see or hear who it might be.

"The last I heard, she was in Africa. The Congo or the Côte d'Ivoire. An attaché to an ambassador or with an NGO or something. But that's just what I've heard. We haven't spoken since high school. I'd thought once or twice about getting in touch with her parents, but…." He shakes his head. "Anyway. We were just kids then."

But this write-off gesture, no one accepts. As a unified voice, his students encourage him to find her, to contact her, it's so easy to track people down these days. They're changing the one rule of their game for him. And for a moment, he believes he can find her. For a moment, he believes he will. Their enthusiasm distracts him from what he was meaning to say. His students applaud the ghosts he's summoned into the world, applaud them back into the memory-grave from which they arose. It appears his will be the last summoning of the night. Moments later, they are all outside under the light of a mercury vapor lamp—the fog has parted and the night is a ladder, a stairway, an open hand—the nightclub's music a muted thud through the walls, and under the light Ben watches their shadows shift and meld as a single shadow, thinking all shadows are one single shadow—just as all light is only the one light—and from this singularity of darkness Ben hears their voices rising and falling, erupting in laughter, and he knows he will never find Naomi. She is lost to him now. Because he loved her, she is lost. It's the one thing he should have said to Rubens in the rehab. The one fact that matters most. Because he loved, he lost.

In the field with the swallows swooping and diving all around him, the dragonflies—black and green and iridescent—would land on him, his arms and shoulders and hair, pausing on him to devour what they'd caught. Anything but invisible. Because he had chosen to, he became central to them. But this is something he does not remember. It's his choice to not remember.

Eventually, his students drift off to their various dorms and apartments, but some insist on walking him home—it's along the way and besides, he's drunk, his legs aren't fully doing his bidding—and though something nags at the back of his mind, it's only after he's smiled and laughed farewell and fumbled his keys into the lock—a wet scrap of pink crepe plastered to the stoop, quivering, almost alive—

after he's pushed the door open and stepped inside that he remembers: he does not want to be here. He cannot risk what is waiting inside. But too late, the closing door's click echoes through the silence inside, and then it too is gone.

Ben stands frozen like a spider in the light. But there's nothing here. Right? Just a bright slice of street light pouring past him, splaying across the cold tile floor. The stairway leading up. His landlady's locked ground-floor apartment door. The fire extinguisher and reel of hose behind a glass door, tucked into a swath of shadow beneath the stairs. There is nothing here. There is nothing here. The world quakes to reveal its feeble edges, its cheap plaster walls, and there is nothing here. Ben takes two steps toward the stairway and it's from that shadowy swath that he sees it emerge—at first it's a man in a square-shouldered suit but it quickly becomes something hunched and horrible, cripple-limbed and cloven-toed—and he reels, spins backward on ungainly legs, and maybe a hand reaches out to strike him or maybe it's the chill fist of the floor that reaches for him, rapping his head stonily into a truer state of darkness than any shadow can know.

He becomes aware first of the sound. Something low between a buzz and a hum. Then there's the light: the unsteady flicker of a fluorescent bulb. Then the morning bell rings and the children surround him, settle into their desks. The scent of pencil shavings and child sweat, the lingering cold from outside. Blue plastic chairs fixed to chipboard desks. Yellow walls plastered with drawings:

lady bugs, spiders, one oil-eyed mantis. The crisp October light through the windows leaks its own living chill. Ben sits still and quiet at his desk. As the bodies fidget into their places. As the tiny voices drop into a murmur. At the head of the room, Ms. Fiori has her hand in the air, an unspoken sign for the students to be silent. Eventually, the classroom complies.

Ben sits amid this, hands folded in lap, not knowing he could be anywhere else.

In her soft early-day alto, Ms. Fiori recites the roll call by memory—"Sandra Adams…? Mark Alotta…? David Babbins…?"—and when no voice responds to the name she's spoken, she spits a length of chalk from her carmine mouth and writes the name on the blackboard. Faintly, Ben remembers having done this himself, countless times holding a pencil in his mouth to imbue life into the words he writes. So that even his silent writing holds the violence of spoken words. But this memory is of an older Ben, pale and uncertain and navigating a world blurred and buffered as if through fog, its reports muffled through an unclosable delay. Less like a memory than a dream he knows he'll have: this version is a future self. He does not worry about what he's seen.

"Ben Nigra…?"

"Present."

And his voice is a child's. And his voice is of a man. He slips his hand into the cubby underneath his desktop and touches a nub of pencil, begins blindly drawing a frail bug-shape on the underside of his desk—long curled limbs, a bulbous raindrop head—nervous without knowing why, but when Ms. Fiori reads Joshua Sams' name, something begins to click.

"…here…."

His friend's voice. Weak and quavering. Giving Ms. Fiori a brief hiccup in her rhythm before continuing down the list. But the hiccup doesn't end for Ben. All through recess, he and Joshua sat side by side on the dew-chilled grass on a small hill above the soccer field while below, the other boys pummeled each other with red rubber balls, screaming. Waiting for the first bell, Joshua hugged his knees to his chest, teeth clenched and neck stiff, and though Ben could sense something big was wrong, neither said a word. The two shared a long morning-cold silence on a hill above the school, and when the bell rang, they lined up with the others to come inside, stash their coats and boots in the classroom closet, and nothing was ever said. As if by not speaking, they could keep a dark something at bay. But now Ben's unspoken worry has been given voice in a single syllable, barely whispered beneath fluorescent light. The silent dark something's been given a name. It's here. Its name is here. Ben's drawing pencil slips from his hand, bounces to the floor. He makes no effort to pick it up.

With roll call complete, Ms. Fiori asks the class to please stand for the pledge of allegiance, and it's as the students start to their feet that a thin animal sound rises above the shuffling. Like the cry of something small being crushed beneath a hoof. Everyone freezes. Nobody stands for the pledge. Turning away from the flag's limp hang, Ms. Fiori gazes into the room, one hand pressed flat above her heart, peers past Ben to the desk beside and behind him.

"Mr. Sams?" All mock-authority. All fear trembling beneath the surface. "Is there something you'd like to share with the rest of the class?" And when Joshua moans again—like there are words in his voice that cannot take shape—Ms. Fiori's spine straightens taut as a guy-line. Every student turns toward the source of the sound, and Ben is helpless but to turn as well.

Hunched over his desk. Skin nearly translucent. Eyes red and rimmed with wet. A slight shake visible through his entire body. But the worst part is that Joshua is looking at him. Ben's certain: he's been staring at him all along. Waiting. His whole body turned toward Ben. Because he cannot move his neck. Ben looks at Joshua and Joshua looks straight back, and everything in his eyes is a plea.

"Would someone please escort Mr. Sams to the nurse's office, please?"

As if she knows exactly what's about to happen and cannot bring herself to face it. A woman so frightened as to ask a child, any child, to do what she herself should do. Across the room, Mark Alotta is already rising from his seat, all smugness and delight at his own helpfulness oozing from his scrubbed-pink face, and at the sight of him, something switches in Ben. What had once been off is now suddenly clicked on. He cannot let Mark Alotta take Joshua away from him. Not again. Like a single frame incised into a steady length of film, Ben can see this moment existing dually, simultaneously. A roll call and a pledge and a soft moan during the morning grammar lesson. A roll call and a pledge interrupted by a louder, more urgent cry. Ben sees his life extending down divergent paths. The countless versions of the world we cannot know. The versions that we can. He stands and tells Ms. Fiori he will go.

"I'll take Joshua," he speaks in the voice of a child.

"Please," he begs in the voice of a man.

Maybe each moment is perfect and unique. Maybe some moments are more perfect than others. Change the world by changing the words.

"Thank you, Ben." Ms. Fiori visibly wilts with relief. Like a cut flower before the blackboard and everyone. "Come back quickly."

Across the room, Mark Alotta sinks back into his seat, his disappointment a near-tangible cloud. Ben stands from his desk and goes to his friend's side. Hooks an arm under Joshua's stiff shoulder, across his stone-straight back. Helps him stand and crosses the room. He does not look back as he opens the heavy classroom door. Together, they step through the other side.

"Thank you," Joshua nearly whispers as the door clicks shut at their backs.

Like a slow fog into a night harbor: it's sinking in.

"Holy shit. Do you realize what we've just done?"

But Joshua doesn't answer, is smiling despite himself, almost laughing through the pain lancing through him, and in his own nervous, disbelieving way, Ben quietly laughs too. They've made it. Through one door, there is only more door. They made it. For the moment, that's all that matters. Still holding onto one another, the boys slowly walk the empty hallway toward the faraway nurse's office.

"I can't believe we did it."

"It couldn't have gone any better, I don't think."

"Are you feeling okay?"

And this time, Joshua laughs for real. "No! Not at all okay."

This isn't precisely the answer Ben had hoped to hear.

"Is there anything else I can do? Any way that maybe…?"

"No," he nearly sighs, his breath weak, shallow. "Some things…."

Along the hallway, their footfalls echo down, echo back, resounding past an unending rosary of doors.

"I don't remember school looking so much like an Escher drawing."

"My guess is, your memory is pretty malleable about now, Benji."

And this time it's Ben who winces as if his insides hurt.

"This isn't real, is it?"

"Were the goblins real?"

"Uh…."

Laughingly, "How about my sister's hand in your hair?"

"Ah, Jesus." It surprises Ben, that he should feel so embarrassed. "You saw that?"

But in response, Joshua only veers them toward one of the classroom doors, stretching on tiptoes to peek through the narrow vertical window above the handle. But they're too short to see much of anything. An undifferentiated field of white. A smooth blankness beyond the glass.

Rolling his eyes theatrically, Joshua shushes between his teeth.

"Bor-ring."

Creeping away from the door, it occurs to Ben there might be a reason that he's here.

"So I guess your sister and I hook up later on."

"I wouldn't worry about it."

"I don't think worrying about it is the problem." Ben bites his lip. "Well. Maybe it is. You're not mad, are you?"

"How can I be mad, Ben? I'll be dead by then."

As if suddenly weaker, Joshua leans more heavily into Ben. But the burden is light. Ben cannot remember if they ever shared such physical closeness when Joshua was still alive.

"Do you remember what it's like? What it'll be like, I mean. Being dead?"

"I guess so. There isn't really much to remember. It's like the kitchen dimmer switch. Everything just kinda fades out."

"And then what?"

"And then nothing, Ben. I'm a Jew. You turn out the lights and wait."

"Wait for what?"

As if it's obvious: "For the World to Come."

Along Ben's spine, a chill fear stutters. He cannot know what answer he was expecting. But a whole other world wasn't it. Yet at the same time, where his arm slings under his friend's shoulder, Ben can feel the warmth of Joshua's pulse. It's just about the most comforting thing he could ever hope to feel.

"I wish I could have done this when it mattered."

"Hey look, a flicker!"

Carefully, Joshua bends down—his body seems looser

now, though still impossibly stiff, as if every muscle had to fight to unclench—and picks up off the floor a plastic bread-bag tab. Worries one inward-turning tooth back and forth until it breaks off. Fits the modified mouth over the meat of one finger and flicks hard, sending the tab spinning like a boomerang through the air. Down the hall, the flicker cants right and hits the wall above a water fountain, drops quietly to the smoothly waxed floor.

"Neat."

"It's good to know I can still do that."

But when they get to the fountain, neither can find where the flicker landed.

"I guess I lose my turn."

"Don't take it too hard."

Up ahead, Ben can see the nurse's office door hanging slightly ajar, thinly drizzling its light, and for one moment, he is both his present and past selves. A child, lost. A tired young man, lost. He cannot pinpoint the difference between the two.

"I keep feeling like I have to get this right." He says the words carefully. As if even in confession, there is no room for error. "Like, if I study this long enough and write enough about it, if I can interview enough people and figure out what went wrong for them, too, I can maybe capture this, make it all okay. It's become a ritual, Josh. If I can learn the motions well enough to see through them, maybe I'll find the key at the center. The thing that holds it all together. It's like I'm casting a spell." And when Joshua laughs: "I'm serious. It's something Rubens used to talk about a lot, how the role of the shaman as healer is to find a way to draw out your devils, sweat them right out of your skin. Because a person's sickness is never just a sickness. It's a demon. The best way to get rid of it is to summon it all the way up. Let it take possession. Burn itself up in a fit of way too much. The person comes out the other side clean. And that's what I'm trying to do. If I say and do everything just right, I can pass through my shadow or let it pass through me, if there even is a difference, and that way maybe I can fix everything that's gone wrong." Without meaning to, he squeezes Joshua tight. Feels his cold ribs against his ribs, the tremble beneath his skin. "*But I don't ever get it right!* It's like the more I try, the more *off* I become. Like I'm erasing everything by trying to fix it."

"Sounds like a Zeno's arrow sort of thing."

"It's not a Zeno's arrow sort of thing."

"It's *exactly* a Zeno's arrow sort of thing."

"I don't think I want to talk about Zeno's arrow, Joshua."

Joshua laughs. "What, does that strike a little too close to home?" He pinches Ben's elbow, gives his shoulder a shake. "That's a joke. A Zeno's arrow joke. You can't ever strike home. You can't even strike."

"This," Ben says, "is not helping, man."

"There's a red deer atop the hill." Joshua's voice is a singsong lilt. "The more you shoot, the more you may."

"Is that some kind of Hebrew thing?"

"It's a riddle, Ben. About the sunrise. But what I don't understand is, why is it so important that you recapture *this?*" Joshua's voice is a wind through autumn limbs. His voice is a shadow in the light. "Why would you want to live any of this again?"

"Because if I don't have this"—and he's shocked to hear himself: he has an answer—"then what else do I have?"

For a moment, the only sound is the echo of their footfalls. The floor tiles' grid-work zooming toward a vanishing point. The speckled acoustic tiles, the repeating measure of doors. All collapsing to vanish at the hall's far-off end. The nurse's office is still no closer than before. This hallway goes on and on.

"You know," Joshua finally says, "how when they point the camera at a TV, so the TV shows a picture of a TV showing a picture of a TV showing a picture of a TV?" He raises one hand to point down the hallway. Classroom doors repeating without end.

"It's not an easy thing to look at."

"TVs inside TVs, Ben. That's us."

"Joshua, I wish—"

"No, Ben. Think about that."

"I don't want—"

But Joshua isn't leaning his weight into him anymore. He's stopped where he stands in the hallway of their school, and his weight is holding Ben still. "Shut up, Ben, for just one second, and think about what I said. You act like you're this amazing listener, but you only ever hear what you want to hear. Listen to something different for once."

"Alright, Jesus!"

"Okay?"

"Okay."

"Okay, then. So do it!"

Ben stares at his friend and sees the screen. Every

screen within each screen. Diminishing into infinity.

"Do you see it, Ben?"

"I do."

Where the screens disappear, he knows: there are always more glowing screens.

"Do you like what you see?"

"Not really. No."

"So maybe you should stop making us live this way. Point the camera somewhere else for a change."

Ben nods and wipes his eyes. But he does not say he will. Smiling sadly, Joshua leans again into his friend, and walking on, Ben is glad for the weight.

"Man, I wish we'd've remembered to set our mantis free."

"Me too! We shouldn't have tried to keep it."

"It's not fair for something to die that way."

But to this, Joshua only shrugs. Looking at his friend, Ben can see Joshua as the man he should have been. Tight curls and lean features. Eyes sharp and limbs long. His confidence and mischief the same exact thing. Always aware of the sun behind the clouds. Ben sees his friend as the child he will always be.

"Josh, was I ever—?" But he can't finish. His throat is a rope twisting from a tree limb, and when Joshua turns to him—all concern and all love shining through his dying white skin and eyes—it's all Ben can do to say, "Was I a good friend? Was I good enough?"

But now, all at once, they're at the open door.

"Was I ever good?"

Ben stands between his friend and the nurse's open

door. Joshua lowers his arm from where he's held it across Ben's back. Takes a single slow step away.

"Good enough for what, Ben?"

But already, this is fading. The light through the open door. The hallway erasing white. Joshua erasing white.

"What more could you have possibly been?"

The doorway behind him and Joshua before him, but in between, Ben is lost and knows: he will always be lost. Why can there never be a peace in this? Because there is no peace in this. Why can there be no end? Ben clenches his eyes shut against the tears, and the light from the hallway and the light from the air burns through him, erases him and dissolves him in light and dissolves him in darkness and when the darkness persists, he opens his burning eyes and is again lying on his apartment building's cold foyer floor while his landlady and her sister hunch over him in the night.

"You think he's dead?"

"He's not dead."

"I think he's dead."

"He's not dead! Look, he's breathing."

"Looks pretty dead."

"No, see, he's looking at us."

"What happened?" Ben tries to sit up but it's like his head is bolted to the floor. He no longer feels drunk. Just sick and dizzy. His stomach a vomitous knot. He rolls onto his side and slowly pushes himself up. "Did you see him?"

"See who?"

"Oh jeez."

"See who?"

"Who is this kid, anyway?"

"There was a man." Faintly, Ben sees Joshua standing alone before the open door. "Someone hit me or something." But already, he knows. His own shadow. Moving through the light cast on the floor. Joshua fades and the dream fades and Ben's left alone with these women and the dark, with his sad awareness of himself.

"This is Ben, a tenant of mine. There weren't no man out here, Ben."

Fleeing from his own shadow. Dreaming of things he can't change.

"You rent to this lunatic? Screaming and crying at the dark like a little girl?"

Both women are short and nightgowned and night-capped. If ever there were goblins in this world…. Ben rolls unsteadily to his feet and lurches toward the stairs.

"Thank you for your help, ladies."

Sleeping on buses. Sleeping standing up. Nothing is changed by a dream.

"You're lifesavers, I swear."

But they follow him up the three flights of stairs, voices grating like wartime machines, and even when they reach his door—with its mail-slot jammed with letters and bills, with the twin blue cardboard boxes propped against the stoop, named and dated, so obvious—these women will not leave him alone. Even as Ben freezes like a pillar of backward-gazing salt. Even as the world sinks and disappears.

His mother's hand in his hair, his head in her lap.

His father resetting the needle.

Flowers falling in an avalanche, always falling.

But this, too, does not last. It occurs to Ben—when things can again occur to Ben—that they want something. So he unlocks the door and steps past the boxes, and these women step over the boxes, step over and into his apartment and will not leave until he's signed a check for this past month's rent and finally, they are gone. Leaving Ben to his empty apartment. Leaving Ben with what he's been avoiding for so long.

Squatting in the entryway, Ben sorts through the mail on his floor. Bills and junk. Fat envelopes from a lawyer. Something from his cousin Elizabeth: a whole other heartbreak in and of itself. He does not need to see these things to know what they are and that they're there.

Ben pushes aside the envelopes and retrieves the boxes from the stoop.

Sets them on the kitchen table.

Slips off the fitted tops.

Stares inside.

He stares for a long time.

It's nearly one o'clock. The first shoreline trains don't run until five. After so many nights spent away from home: what's one more night? Ben adds the contents of one box to the other. Shimmies on the top and fits the box under his arm. Heads out to wait on the streets. In the dark empty stretches where all the storefronts are hidden behind drop-down gates of corrugated metal. Where vacant lots glitter with glass capturing the street light. Where the factory flames stain everything with smoke. His shape reflected in all darkened windows, his shadow imprinted on all sidewalks by all street lamps, by any passing car, long and disfigured and tied forever to his feet. It doesn't matter where he goes because everywhere is the same. Ben exits into the welcome anonymity of night.

FIELD AND MARSH AND VAST TRACTS OF FARMLAND. LOW STANDS of trees. A mineral refinery. Outside Ben's window, the landscape races past while inside the surface train, he barely feels he's moving. Clean white sunlight unobstructed by clouds. He's certain, there's warmth out there.

The train stops and with his powder blue box, Ben deboards onto a platform. White sand and severe grass. A road bisecting a wide, open space. The distant sound of flocking birds calling. Far off, Ben can see the pink crown of pale rocks but from the platform, there are no people and there are no houses. An empty parking lot and an empty station alongside an empty road. Among the platform's white-painted cement pillars, long ribbons of crepe paper tangle and flutter. Pink and white and blue. The train pulls away and Ben steps down, crosses the road to a narrow boardwalk leading toward the water.

Land reserved by the state, this is where the savvy locals will come in the summer. To beat the crowds. To watch birds and watch the water. Explore cliffs or stretch out on the slim, sandy beach. But that won't be for a month or more. Ben passes through the phalanx of shivering grey-green grass to the pounding shore, a wishbone of sand curtailed by whaleback stone to the right, by rising dinosaur cliffs to the left. Deep blue water capped in white like storm waves in a painting, perpetually crashing in.

The one change, Ben noticed right away. When they were finished and Naomi left to clean up in the bathroom, Ben crossed naked to where his handmade card hung on the bedroom wall. Yellow and purple and red. He took down the card and flipped it over, gazing at the one word that'd been pressed against the wall all these years. The apology of a child too lost to know what he was sorry for. Ben pressed the one word to his mouth. Touched his lips to everything he'd ever meant to say. Where the water meets the earth, Ben stands staring through the distant horizon as if considering an idea barely forming at the edge of his waking mind. A screen within a screen within a screen. He turns toward the pink granite cliffs rising like a temple to his left.

He knows there's an easier way. If he backtracked, he could take the trail spurring off from the boardwalk. Gradually mount the cliff's knuckled spine. Find himself easily at the peak, but no. Maneuvering over the steep jags of stone—sometimes, perilously, terrifyingly, resting the box on an upper shelf so he can pull himself up—Ben slowly ascends the cliffside, past shattered shells and crippled junipers with barely a toe-hold in the rocks, but eventually the pitch slackens, rounds off, and when he reaches the top, the wind off the water is the cool ruffling hand of a rough but caring god. The water has no end before him and the earth has no end behind him and Ben stands between the two with the wind whipping his hair, his open jacket, his very breath.

This took more out of him than he'd expected. He's shaky up here, legs rubbery, head swimming as he unsteadily crosses the bald rock dome, seeking an edge.

But each precipice he finds leads only to another lower precipice. Having reached the top, he must again descend until finally he's perched on a ledge above the roiling water so far below, legs hanging freely with the powder-blue box resting in his lap like some contented, sleeping thing. Ben leans into the wind and wipes his face and waits for his breath to return.

It was less than a month ago that his mom had her accident. Boxing up old books in the upstairs hallway to bring to the local Goodwill, she sprang to answer a ringing phone. Tripped over the box. Tumbled so gracelessly down the stairs. Her coma was a floodlight, all the world beyond its blinding flare negated into depthless shadow. What other choice did his father's heart have? After it quit, Ben quit too and now he has this box and a house in his hometown and everything inside is still untouched but at least they're all together now. The happy family reunited. Two bodies in one box. One box and one body on a cliff above a water repeating ineffably its name forever.

Slowly, softly, like something might break, Ben eases the top off the box. The wind immediately rends the boxtop from his hands, sucks it tumbling to the greeting waves and shattered shells below. He watches the top bobbing in the water—a tiny lost ship—until he cannot see it anymore.

Unwinding the wire-tied bag, he rolls back the edges and stares inside. A stratifying line divides the two ashes, one slightly darker than the other, but not remembering who he poured into whom—the name printed on the lid equally lost to the water below—he cannot tell who is who.

"Sorry, guys."

He sinks his hand into their bodies. Spreads his fingers through what was once their hair, once their lungs. Their bones and toenails. The plaque of their teeth. When he pulls his hand free, he cups some of each of them in his shaking palm.

The day of his mom's fall, he had called and no one answered. He'd wanted to tell her about the botanical gardens. The laughing azalea woman who smelled like burnt toast. The bumble bee's ricochet off the Hawaiian-shirt guy. The cherry blossoms' gentle rain. Wanted to tell her for no other reason than because these things made him happy. He wonders if she heard his call.

The first handful rises as a helix in the wind. The second puffs and disburses, catches the sunlight in a silvery flare, is gone. The third sinks. But already, his hand is sinking, too. Like his strength is vanishing with each dissolving cloud of ash. His whole body melting into the rocks. He can almost feel it, the deep hum of the world pulsing through him. But is it ridiculous or divine? It's both. It's all he can do not to fall off the ledge. What makes it ridiculous is it's divine.

He takes a handful of ash and rubs it into his hair.

He rubs ash across his face.

Into the collar-sweat of his neck.

The soft pink flesh of his tongue.

The scent is like the natural fertilizers his mother would sow in her flowerbeds—blood meal for nitrogen, bone meal for phosphorous—but the taste is nothing. A negation. A negative. Like the inverse of a photograph from which the photograph is made.

He rolls a tiny bone bit on his ashy tongue then spits it

into the water below, coughs and chokes, already regretting what he's done. Regretting all things he's ever done. But with the bone spat and the long history that's led to this moment, what more wrong can he do? He pulls out the bag and jettisons the box, shakes out the bag like a sandy sheet, ash billowing everywhere then dispelled into the vast everything else of the world, and immediately he knows what further wrongs exist. No wonder laughing looks so much like crying. He should have saved something. There should have been something to save.

But the wind blows the ash from his hair, from his skin. Moist grey clumps caked beneath his eyes. His mouth sloughs the ash from itself, and he swallows, and it's gone. The effort to hold on is equal to the effort to let go and when he does, the empty bag floats off like a parachute or balloon. Almost weightless. A whispering shush. Drifting safely down.

Across the infinite spaces, the sun continues its course and the earth continues its course and the moon pulls the water below to crash and be still, crash and be still. Ben allows the numbness within him to simply become him. Crash and be still. A wash of pure light that is also a door. He allows himself to gradually awaken. And then: he is awake. The cry of birds. The whistling wind. Water rinsing pink stone. A music identical forward as in reverse. Every-thing exactly the same. In the slow sureness of someone who knows he has nowhere to go, Ben rises from the cliff face and descends to the sand. Crosses the grassy space. Waits along the tracks with the tangled crepe ribbon for his returning engine to come.

The first draft of this novel began in a several-hundred-year-old church in Moretta, Italy in the January of 2010, in the sleepy company of my friend (and eventual publisher) Patrick Kiley, and was finished that following summer while cat-sitting Fernace for Burdie Burd in her apartment in Portland, Maine. In between, some small portions were written at my oldest sister's home and while barhopping with Kristen Ellis in coastal Oregon. During the months and years of editing and rewriting, I benefitted enormously from the invaluable insight of several early readers, namely Jacob Cholak, Megan Grumbling, Anne Danae, and Justin Woollard, and somewhere amid all this, Andy Lyman (also an eventual publisher) and I collaborated on an interactive hypertext version of the first chapter. The late Matthew Underwood first introduced me to the film *Little Fugitive*, which left me deeply stunned for, well, ever. Genevieve Johnson has throughout been the most steadfast balustrade, keeping me working and upright (oftentimes literally) in all of the most vital ways, and Mark Priola, Derek Kimball, and Scott Sell have remained unwavering in their support, even when my actions seem most unreasonable and alien to their sensibilities. And now, by publishing *Our Shadows' Voice*, Donna Bister and Marc Estrin have given me at-long-last permission to finally cease agonizing over each word in each scene, each minute tic of dialogue, and leave these poor imagined people be. This cumulative assist has me perpetually grateful for all of these people who, for no practical gain, have gifted me with their time and their patience and their compassion. In a world of stony raisins, you are the most supple grapes.

(Author photo by Ed Dittenhoefer)

Douglas W. Milliken is the author of the novel *To Sleep as Animals*, the collection *Blue of the World*, and several chapbooks and collaborative multimedia projects, including *In the Mines* with the musician Scott Sell and *Monolith* with the metal smith Cat Bates. He is the recipient of a Pushcart Prize and a Maine Literary Award, along with prizes from *Glimmer Train*, the *Stoneslide Corrective*, and RA & Pin Drop Studios. He lives with his domestic and creative partner, Genevieve Johnson, in the industrial riverscape of Saco, Maine.

About Fomite

A fomite is a medium capable of transmitting infectious organisms from one individual to another.

"The activity of art is based on the capacity of people to be infected by the feelings of others." Tolstoy, *What Is Art?*

Writing a review on Amazon, Good Reads, Shelfari, Library Thing or other social media sites for readers will help the progress of independent publishing. To submit a review, go to the book page on any of the sites and follow the links for reviews. Books from independent presses rely on reader-to-reader communications.

For more information or to order any of our books, visit:
http://www.fomitepress.com/our-books.html

More Titles from Fomite...

Novels
Joshua Amses — During This, Our Nadir
Joshua Amses — Ghatsr
Joshua Amses — Raven or Crow
Joshua Amses — The Moment Before an Injury
Jaysinh Birjepatel — Nothing Beside Remains
Jaysinh Birjepatel — The Good Muslim of Jackson Heights
David Brizer — Victor Rand
Paula Closson Buck — Summer on the Cold War Planet
Dan Chodorkoff — Loisaida
David Adams Cleveland — Time's Betrayal
Jaimee Wriston Colbert — Vanishing Acts
Roger Coleman — Skywreck Afternoons
Marc Estrin — Hyde
Marc Estrin — Kafka's Roach
Marc Estrin — Speckled Vanities
Zdravka Evtimova — In the Town of Joy and Peace
Zdravka Evtimova — Sinfonia Bulgarica
Daniel Forbes — Derail This Train Wreck
Greg Guma — Dons of Time
Richard Hawley — The Three Lives of Jonathan Force
Lamar Herrin — Father Figure
Michael Horner — Damage Control
Ron Jacobs — All the Sinners Saints
Ron Jacobs — Short Order Frame Up
Ron Jacobs — The Co-conspirator's Tale
Scott Archer Jones — And Throw Away the Skins
Scott Archer Jones — A Rising Tide of People Swept Away
Julie Justicz — Degrees of Difficulty
Maggie Kast — A Free Unsullied Land
Darrell Kastin — Shadowboxing with Bukowski
Coleen Kearon — #triggerwarning
Coleen Kearon — Feminist on Fire

Fomite

Jan English Leary — Thicker Than Blood
Diane Lefer — Confessions of a Carnivore
Rob Lenihan — Born Speaking Lies
Douglas W. Milliken — Our Shadows' Voice
Colin Mitchell — Roadman
Ilan Mochari — Zinsky the Obscure
Peter Nash — Parsimony
Peter Nash — The Perfection of Things
George Ovitt — Stillpoint
George Ovitt — Tribunal
Gregory Papadoyiannis — The Baby Jazz
Pelham — The Walking Poor
Andy Potok — My Father's Keeper
Frederick Ramey — Comes A Time
Joseph Rathgeber — Mixedbloods
Kathryn Roberts — Companion Plants
Robert Rosenberg — Isles of the Blind
Fred Russell — Rafi's World
Ron Savage — Voyeur in Tangier
David Schein — The Adoption
Lynn Sloan — Principles of Navigation
L.E. Smith — The Consequence of Gesture
L.E. Smith — Travers' Inferno
L.E. Smith — Untimely RIPped
Bob Sommer — A Great Fullness
Tom Walker — A Day in the Life
Susan V. Weiss —My God, What Have We Done?
Peter M. Wheelwright — As It Is On Earth
Suzie Wizowaty — The Return of Jason Green

Poetry

Anna Blackmer — Hexagrams
Antonello Borra — Alfabestiario
Antonello Borra — AlphaBetaBestiaro
Antonello Borra — The Factory of Ideas
L. Brown — Loopholes
Sue D. Burton — Little Steel
David Cavanagh— Cycling in Plato's Cave
James Connolly — Picking Up the Bodies
Greg Delanty — Loosestrife
Mason Drukman — Drawing on Life
J. C. Ellefson — Foreign Tales of Exemplum and Woe
Tina Escaja/Mark Eisner — Caida Libre/Free Fall
Anna Faktorovich — Improvisational Arguments
Barry Goldensohn — Snake in the Spine, Wolf in the Heart
Barry Goldensohn — The Hundred Yard Dash Man
Barry Goldensohn — The Listener Aspires to the Condition of Music
R. L. Green — When You Remember Deir Yassin
Gail Holst-Warhaft — Lucky Country
Raymond Luczak — A Babble of Objects
Kate Magill — Roadworthy Creature, Roadworthy Craft

Fomite

Tony Magistrale — Entanglements
Gary Mesick — General Discharge
Andreas Nolte — Mascha: The Poems of Mascha Kaléko
Sherry Olson — Four-Way Stop
Brett Ortler — Lessons of the Dead
Aristea Papalexandrou/Philip Ramp — Μας προσπερνά/It's Overtaking Us
Janice Miller Potter — Meanwell
Janice Miller Potter — Thoreau's Umbrella
Philip Ramp — The Melancholy of a Life as the Joy of Living It Slowly Chills
Joseph D. Reich — A Case Study of Werewolves
Joseph D. Reich — Connecting the Dots to Shangrila
Joseph D. Reich — The Derivation of Cowboys and Indians
Joseph D. Reich — The Hole That Runs Through Utopia
Joseph D. Reich — The Housing Market
Kenneth Rosen and Richard Wilson — Gomorrah
Fred Rosenblum — Vietnumb
David Schein — My Murder and Other Local News
Harold Schweizer — Miriam's Book
Scott T. Starbuck — Carbonfish Blues
Scott T. Starbuck — Hawk on Wire
Scott T. Starbuck — Industrial Oz
Seth Steinzor — Among the Lost
Seth Steinzor — To Join the Lost
Susan Thomas — In the Sadness Museum
Susan Thomas — The Empty Notebook Interrogates Itself
Paolo Valesio/Todd Portnowitz — La Mezzanotte di Spoleto/Midnight
in Spoleto
Sharon Webster — Everyone Lives Here
Tony Whedon — The Tres Riches Heures
Tony Whedon — The Falkland Quartet
Claire Zoghb — Dispatches from Everest

Stories
Jay Boyer — Flight
L. M Brown — Treading the Uneven Road
Michael Cocchiarale — Here Is Ware
Michael Cocchiarale — Still Time
Neil Connelly — In the Wake of Our Vows
Catherine Zobal Dent — Unfinished Stories of Girls
Zdravka Evtimova — Carts and Other Stories
John Michael Flynn — Off to the Next Wherever
Derek Furr — Semitones
Derek Furr — Suite for Three Voices
Elizabeth Genovise — Where There Are Two or More
Andrei Guriuanu — Body of Work
Zeke Jarvis — In A Family Way
Arya Jenkins — Blue Songs in an Open Key
Jan English Leary — Skating on the Vertical
Marjorie Maddox — What She Was Saying
William Marquess — Boom-shacka-lacka
Gary Miller — Museum of the Americas
Jennifer Anne Moses — Visiting Hours

Fomite

Martin Ott — Interrogations
Christopher Peterson — Amoebic Simulacra
Jack Pulaski — Love's Labours
Charles Rafferty — Saturday Night at Magellan's
Ron Savage — What We Do For Love
Fred Skolnik— Americans and Other Stories
Lynn Sloan — This Far Is Not Far Enough
L.E. Smith — Views Cost Extra
Caitlin Hamilton Summie — To Lay To Rest Our Ghosts
Susan Thomas — Among Angelic Orders
Tom Walker — Signed Confessions
Silas Dent Zobal — The Inconvenience of the Wings

Odd Birds
William Benton — Eye Contact: Writing on Art
Micheal Breiner — the way none of this happened
J. C. Ellefson — Under the Influence: Shouting Out to Walt
David Ross Gunn — Cautionary Chronicles
Andrei Guriuanu and Teknari — The Darkest City
Gail Holst-Warhaft — The Fall of Athens
Roger Lebovitz — A Guide to the Western Slopes and the Outlying
                    Area
Roger Lebovitz — Twenty-two Instructions for Near Survival
dug Nap— Artsy Fartsy
Delia Bell Robinson — A Shirtwaist Story
Peter Schumann — A Child's Deprimer
Peter Schumann — Belligerent & Not So Belligerent Slogans from
                    the Possibilitarian Arsenal
Peter Schumann — Bread & Sentences
Peter Schumann — Charlotte Salomon
Peter Schumann — Diagonal Man, Volumes One and Two
Peter Schumann — Faust 3
Peter Schumann — Planet Kasper, Volumes One and Two
Peter Schumann — We

Plays
Stephen Goldberg — Screwed and Other Plays
Michele Markarian — Unborn Children of America

Essays
Robert Sommer — Losing Francis: Essays on the Wars at Home